India Lockdown
A War against Corona

Satish Saykar

Copyright © 2021 Satish Saykar

All rights reserved.

ISBN: 9798508354541

In the memory of those
who lost their lives because of Corona Pandemic
and
All the Corona Warriors
who fought against it.

If you make mistakes
you will be criticized,
Try to correct yourself,
don't torture the critics.

Section 1

1

Chinese things are generally duplicate and temporary for use, but this virus was something different. Permanent. Ever dying. It was surprising that the country which makes the cheap things that could live for a short while only can produce such a virus that can swallow the whole world.

Today was the fourth day of lockdown. I got up early in the morning. There was nothing to do in urgency. So I preferred to lie down on the mattress. After a long time, the curiosity let me out of the bed and I switched on the TV to see the news related to Corona. I was interested to know what happened in India or in Maharashtra. The world had already totally trapped in the jaws of Corona.

I found the news of what the NGOs were doing to help the people who had nothing to eat due to the lockdown. The people who earn very less had to live without meal. They were the first victims of lockdown policy declared by the government. The government only knew that the total lockdown was the only solution to stop the disease. But nobody had thought of those who are beggars, nomads, unemployed or temporary employed.

On the 31st January, 2020, there were found three Corona positive patients. But the government did not take it seriously. The people were going abroad and coming back. The Government of India had no insight in future as a result of which it was not guessed what will happen next.

We used to listen many stories and case studies of what had happened in Wuhan, China, Italy and other European countries. We also heard of strict lockdown in Wuhan. The video clips, where the windows and doors were packed from outside; so nobody could come out of their houses, were used to come on the WhatsApp and on the News Channels as well. Nobody was talking of the possibility of lockdown in India. Three people were infected, of course. It was thought that they had come from China, so are they affected. All of us were sure that it won't spread more.

In the second week of March, the discussion started in India. Most of the news channels and politicians had expressed the need to stop this disease; otherwise, it would be difficult to control. There may be a loss of lives in lakhs or crores. The government is the parent of its people. The government said on 13th March, 2020 that there will be holidays to schools and colleges to avoid the spread of Corona virus. It was a time when the board examinations of S.S.C. were going on. So the government declared that the examinations will continue, they won't be stopped.

The next two-three days were very critical for us. The universities and the governments declared the holidays. Accordingly, we received the notices from Sangli and Kolhapur districts specifying that there will be holiday up to 25th March. The reason was also clear. The university examinations were to start from 27th March. The government orders were very clear that the University examinations will be continued as per the schedule. Everybody was of the opinion that at least for ten days the schools and colleges will remain closed. The government also issued the notice for the teachers that they should continue their work from home and must be present at the work place so that they can go to the college as and when they are needed. So in Sangli and Kolhapur, all colleges and schools were closed. Only the board examinations were continued.

But our District Collector had issued a corrigendum stating that the teachers in schools and colleges must be present in their schools and colleges. It means the holidays are only for the students. Does he mean that teachers won't be affected by the disease? On the very next day, University and College Teachers' Association, District authorities wrote to the Collector about the university and governments circular regarding 'work from home.' Unfortunately, he did not replied in any way.

So as an Assistant Professor, we have to be in the college. The sentence 'university examinations would continue as per the schedule' was interpreted differently. We were conducting the Preliminary Examinations in our college. It is a part of an internal evaluation or say a trick used by the college administration to collect the funds. The students have to pay the examination fees. But it doesn't end here. Those students who remain absent have to pay fine according to the rules designed by the college and those who are present but fail in the examination are also fined. It's a milking cow for the college.

The preliminary examinations were going on. Our Principal was of the opinion that examinations have not been banned. The teachers in private were talking on the issue that the Principal had misinterpreted the term 'university examinations'. So we could not declare holidays for the students. The students in the era of WhatsApp, Facebook and Twitter know everything. They started chatting in their own groups out of which one said:

They don't care if we die.
They only know collecting money from us.

Teachers and especially those who have good salaries can never revolt against the system. So the examinations continued. Two days later, everywhere there was a discussion on Corona and its spread. Finally, the authorities thought over the issue and feared if anybody gets affected; the college may have to pay the price. The college may be taken responsible for the mishap. So the Principal issued a notice on Monday, 16th March, 2020 that the preliminary examination of all the classes has been postponed up to 1st April, 2020. But he cleared that the presence of teachers was must in the college.

Our college had created what's app group of its teachers. The circulars regarding the orders of holidays were posted by the teachers. Some of them were asking the question whether to attend the college or not. The Principal became angry at all this. He called the meeting of all the heads and the Vice-Principals. In a meeting, he used a harsh and inappropriate language for the teachers. All of a sudden one of the teachers present there stood up and asked the Principal as to why he was using such an inappropriate language and warned him not to use such a bad language while addressing the teachers. Then he calmed down. So he issued an oral notice that the teachers should attend the college and prepare the well documented files to be submitted to the Internal Quality Assurance Cell. All the teachers followed his guidelines. Two days later, I was called by the Principal in his cabin. In an informal discussion, he said:

"The teachers are mad and unworthy."

I was shocked to listen it. I waited for his further comments. He continued:

"You might have got holidays, but you people are very fool. 1200 people went to *Kaas* Plateau on the same day the holiday was declared. That's why the Collector took the decision that the teachers should present at their workplace. And the holiday was declared for the students only."

"It's nothing, but the whim of the Collector. But he will be cross-questioned in the near future. He will have to answer as to why he has taken such a wrong decision. What is the difference between Satara and other districts coming under Shivaji University, Kolhapur." I said.

He said: "You can't talk in this way. He is a responsible officer."

I answered, "He will have to face in future if Corona spreads and any mishap takes place."

He stopped the discussion. But he might have thought on what I said. Further investigation, responsibility and so on. On the next day, he took a meeting of the staff and declared that there will be holiday till you receive a phone call or message from the college.

2

On 19th March, 2020 in the evening, perhaps, the Hon. Prime Minister Narendra Modi addressed the nation where he ordered to keep '*Janata Curfew*' on 22nd March, 2020. He advised all the citizens not to go out of home for a day. He added that people should come out in the balcony or terrace or out of the front door at 5.00 p.m. and clap or ring the bell or make sound with the help of the plates to increase the confidence of those doctors, nurses and police officers who were helping the people in fighting against the Corona virus. This was the mission called '*Taali Bajao, Thaali Bajao, Ghanti Bajao.*'

Calamities do not come alone. In the last week, I had many turns to the hospital. My whole family had suffered from cough and fever. On 20th March, 2020, the doctor diagnosed that I was perhaps suffering from Malariya and he gave me the medicines accordingly. It means I was supposed to be in house at least for four days. On 22nd March, 2020 we strictly followed '*Janata Curfew*' and at 5.00 p.m., we went on the terrace to clap for the Corona Warriors. A very big sound of claps, bells and plates came from all sides. My children also took plates and spoons in their hands and started beating it with enthusiasm. All of us celebrated the day as per the directions of our Prime Minister.

After some time, the government of Maharashtra declared lockdown in whole Maharashtra to fight against Corona and all the homes in Maharshtra were transformed in to jails for its members. Still, it was fun to be at homes with the family members, nobody is allowed to go out without any valid reason. I do not remember I had lived for few days with my wife and children without any touch with the outside world in the last thirteen years. My children were also happy because I was there to accompany them. I asked them that the holidays given to them were for study. So study regularly at least for some time became mandatory for them. For the first two days, my children used to play with the children in the neighbourhood. They were happy for I was with them. My daughter asked me:

"Baba, how long will you be with us"?
"Till the lockdown ends."
"How long will it continue"?
"Can't say for sure"?

I saw happiness on her face that cannot be explained in words. We had thought that up to 25th March, 2020 the lockdown will be over. But on 24th March, 2020 the Prime Minister Narendra Modi had addressed the nation for the second time and asked the fellow citizens to lock themselves in their homes. He declared a lockdown for twenty-one days. It was a shock for me. I thought of going to the native place; but my wife said it would be dangerous to go there in such condition. She claimed that we have easy availability of health facilities. In the native place, we will be in the farm. May be we have to face some problems there.

Along with this, in mean time, the college issued a notice stating that the co-editors of the College Magazine should work efficiently and return the manuscripts well proof-read within two days from the date of receiving. As I was the co-editor of English

Section and the order of 'Work from Home', I thought it better to stay in the city where I was teaching. If I am called to the college, I shall reach there within five minutes; but if I go to my native place, how shall I come back. So I left the thought of going to my native place.

As the lockdown was declared by the government, the bus and railway services were stopped. Here the problem started. On the first day of lockdown, I visited the city to buy some grocery and the sack of wheat so that there would be no problem for the twenty-one days. Though I had left the home for shop, I was little bit frightened. I doubted whether the police would beat me and send me back. Most of the times, it happens that you are punished in such circumstances when there is no fault of yours. So I entered the city not by the usually crowded road, but went through the outskirts of the city. The main shutter of the shop was closed. All other visible shops were closed. I thought the shop was closed; but on the next moment, I saw that the shop was opened from its side door. I entered the shop and purchased the required things.

On the way back home, I decided to go by the main road to know the condition in the city. In *Azad Chowk*, there was a barricades placed by the police. Two policemen with masks on their face were sitting on the chair having canes in their hands. I was afraid, but they did not stop me. I saw almost all the shops were closed. The government declared that the grocery shops, petrol pumps, hospitals and other essential services will be open. But most of the small grocery shops were locked. Petrol pumps were opened, but they had stopped issuing petrol to the common people. Only on duty people were given petrol. Thank God. At least the hospitals and medical shops were open.

When I was in home, I took the study of my son for some time. He was very happy for that. Up to this time I had never taught him for more than ten minutes; but on that day, I spent almost two hours with him. My daughter, very sincere in study, always wanted me to teach her; but her sincerity became the root cause that I did not taught her. I know very well though I do not teach her, she will do it on her own. She said,

"Baba, you haven't taught me like this"?

"Beta, teaching is needed in case of dull only," I said.

My son silently looked at me, laughed then and started his study again. I was also happy for I had the time to teach my son. Then I wasted most of my time in watching the same news on different channels. It had changed the atmosphere at home. Even the children were talking freely and like the scholars at home on Corona. Everywhere, there were words: *"Stay home, stay safe."*

In the evening, some neighbouring children came to my house and asked my son to play with them. I was to allow him, but my wife came forward and said to go back saying that Corona is there, so don't play. Live at home. I tried to tell her but she told me back that I should be rather strict with the children; otherwise, there will be problem for all of us. This is a contagious disease. Don't take it easy. I was quiet.

When there was dark, I went on the terrace of the home with all family members. We played together for some time. We had a meal together. Watching a TV or reading the books was the only way available to us due to lockdown.

3

It was the 2nd day of lockdown on 26th March, 2020. I got up early in the morning. We enjoyed the breakfast and helped my son in learning Mathematics. Everyday new number of Corona patients, only the change in number. The talks on TV limited to Corona. Only positive thing happened was the news that the Corona patients were cured and sent back to their homes. Even the hospital nurses and doctors gave farewell to those patients by giving them a big applause by going on the road.

Now one thing was sure. It increased my confidence. I showed the news on Youtube to my wife. I hoped that she will welcome the news. But her response was different. She said, "Though the patients are getting cured, we should not go out." Showing the news to her was misinterpreted by her that I wanted the children to go out. So she reacted in a very different way than I hoped for.

In the evening, I had to go to bring milk. I had to go at least one Kilometre away. I thought to fill the fuel in the two-wheeler. I stopped the vehicle on the petrol pump and asked for the petrol of one hundred rupees; but the person asked whether I was on duty. I said, 'No.' Then he said, "We have been ordered not to give petrol to anyone other than the persons on duty. You have to bring the recommendation letter from the government officials." What does it mean? Everywhere the media and the government were saying that petrol pumps are open. What is its use? The government said that the people are allowed to go out to bring the essential things. Then how will they go? Or do they want us to go by foot? I left the pump and went towards the house of milkman. On the way, I found the big stones placed on the road to block it. I stopped. There I saw a boy.

"There is no milk. Nobody will give you milk. It is stopped." He said.

"I'm not going for milk." I said.

Then he said nothing. I reached the milkman where a woman, maybe she was a relative of the milkman, asked how could I reached there. Did the police do not stop me? I was shocked. It means the police was there on the blocked road. I talked with the milkman.

"Till it was okay, I'll come for milk. Otherwise I won't come till the lockdown ends. I don't want to get in trouble."

"Here is no problem. You can come and take the milk."

I took the milk and returned home. On the third day of lockdown, I got up late in the morning. Due to lockdown, I had nothing to do. Just to pass the time. I woke up all the members. We all did Yoga to be fit in those days. Then we had our breakfast. I turned the TV on. The news again focussing on the same issue: 'Stay home, stay fit.' I was watching the news by heart to know the present status of the disease. The disease was spreading day by day. It created a feeling of uneasiness. Suddenly, the cell phone ranged. The person on the other end was my colleague in social movement. I asked his how about but he told me the news of death of our friend's mother. It was a shock for me. I assured him that I shall go to his house. He said that he would not reach for the funeral as the lockdown was going on. I told him that I will definitely go there.

I told the news to my wife and children. The first spontaneous words came out of my wife's mouth.

"You don't go."

She knew very well how close our friendship was. When a close friends mother dies, what the other one will do. He will stay in the friend's family for a maximum time. But the time was different. There was a danger even in helping others. So she was right. After all she was my wife. What else one can expect from her?

I told her that I shall come back within half an hour. I called one of my friends to inform him about the death that took place in our friend's house. We together went to the friend's house. We reached there and touched the feet of the dead. There were few people around us. Most of them hid their faces by the handkerchiefs or masks. There was a tension present everywhere. Suddenly, there came horning two-wheeler of police. They looked doubtfully. When one of them saw the preparations of funeral, he just said,

"Keep distance. Take care."

The bike left then. The friendship was very close; but Corona had made a distance between us. I just looked at him. I did neither try to console my friend nor his family. Instead I stood out of the house on the road to save myself from Corona. After some time, my friend came out and stood by my side under the hot son, leaving the dead and her son to suffer alone. There was some time needed for the guests to come. So we had to wait for the funeral.

We then sat in the nearby building under construction to maintain the social distance. After waiting for almost for an hour, we got tired of waiting. Still the guests had not arrived. We decided to go home before the funeral because we also feared.

My wife had placed two buckets full of water on the terrace. I washed my clothes and bathed afterwards. Having lunch, I thought myself that if there was no fear of Corona, perhaps I would have spent almost two-three whole days there only, may have come home only to eat. The need of social distancing had resulted into psychological distancing as well. So I left my friend with his dead mother.

After I posted a message on WhatsApp groups to inform other friends about the death that took place in my friend's house. Some of my friends preferred to express sorrow on what's app wall only. Some called me and stated their inability to attend any of the funeral rites due to the lockdown. I questioned myself, "whether the country is locked down or the minds"?

Anyway, it is said that you can win the world, if you live on. So everybody tried to save one's life. In the evening, the news came on the television that Doordarshan will start showing *Ramayana* in the morning and evening at nine and everyday two parts will be shown regularly. Also DD Bharati started broadcasting *Mahabharat*. Was it the need of time? Definitely not. All the temples were closed, mosques were sealed, nobody was allowed in churches and gurudwaras. They were turned into no man's land. We Indians are rather silly. When the good things happen, we give its credit to the God. If any mishap takes place, we say that the God is punishing us. Both the times, the God is credited. It is also said that whenever the anti-religious things happen and the religion or good people are in danger, the God takes birth on the earth. Every mishap or calamity is taken as the punishment given to us by God.

The government had taken the decision to indulge people at home. Many leaders and media members started congratulating the government for taking such a good step. Few people talked against it, but their voices were suppressed.

I watched the *Ramayana* Part-I with my family members. Spent an hour watching the TV, I posted a comment on a WhatsApp group 'Ram is back. Whenever the government is in danger, Ram is called for help.' It was the fourth day of lockdown. The number of Corona infected in India was 945 out of which 167 cases were found in Maharashtra.

The government has taken the decision of lockdown; but did not think of those workers who were away from home. Most of them were gypsies or nomads. The people, poor people without work did not have anything to eat. At some places, the food was provided by NGOs and GOs; but it was a drop fell in the desert. What was their crime? Why were they locked? Why their jobs were taken away? Who is to be blamed for depriving them from bread and butter? What shall they do in such a situation?

The workers from Bihar and Uttar Pradesh are on their way to native place. They had been to Maharashtra, Madhya Pradesh, Gujrat, Delhi, Rajasthan in search of work. Due to lockdown, their lives were transferred in hail. They could do nothing. They were helpless. They were on the way to their native place; but the bus and railway transport was closed. They were left with no way to these people. At last they started their journey on feet. Their journey was not a walking distance; but they have to cross the distance of hundreds of kilometres without food to eat and water to drink. Where will they stay? What about the security of women?

The government had taken many efforts to bring rich people from abroad to India; but they had not given enough time for the poor to settle themselves and taken the decision of lockdown. If they had taken enough care in February, if all the flights had been cancelled or the people returned from foreign countries compulsory quarantined, then the things might have been very different. But we have different rules for different people. The rich people always enjoy the special status.

Kanika Kapoor, the celebrity, had come to India from abroad; but she saved herself from the medical check-up on the airport. She did not go to her house; but she lived in a hotel, participated in various grand parties. She was so special that she participated in parties which consist of the Health Minister of Uttar Pradesh, the former Chief Minister, Rajasthan; her son and many others. This was not enough; but the person in her contact went to the parliament and even visited the President's House. Thank God, the President had not shaken hands with him. The people, who had participated in the party in which Kanika Kapoor was present, had to quarantine themselves afterwards.

4

29th March, 2020. Lockdown Day-V. It was the third day after the death of my friend's mother. I was supposed to be there to attend the funeral rites. I got up early in the morning. I expected a call from one of my friends. Friend, anyone, other than whose mother died. It was 8 o' clock in the morning. Nobody called me. After the morning exercise, I took bath. Still there was confusion in the mind. It was like Hamlet, 'To attend or not attend the funeral.' The reason was simple. Corona virus spread. My wife asked what I was thinking. I told her about my plan to attend the funeral. She said,

> "There is no need to go, because there will be many people. Don't hurl yourself in danger. Better go on any other day to meet your friend."

Her idea was not bad; I could not stop my confusion. Then I thought if any of my friend calls me, I shall attend the funeral rites; otherwise I won't go.

WhatsApp and television were the only alternatives to pass the time. Otherwise, teach the son or work on computer. I opened the WhatsApp and found the message that raised a question about the progressive people in Maharashtra. The post explained that all the progressive people had left the ground during the Corona epidemic and the central government along with the volunteers of R.S.S. was working continuously for the nation. I was surprised. How naive these people were? They had lost their ability to think on their own. They had become blind. They do not see the reality. They only know what the media shows or prints. So I posted a comment as a reply to it.

> *He had imported Corona in India. If the airports had been locked down a month before and those who came to India compulsory quarantined, no need of lockdown was there.*

After some time, I received a video message which said that Modi had brought those who were living in foreign countries to India with honour by sending aeroplanes. But the poor workers spread all over India were being beaten severely. The government spent lakhs of rupees on the Corona patients imported from the foreign countries and the poor people were left to die without food to eat and transport facility to travel. Why did these people go abroad? What do they do there? All the time blaming for uncleanliness, insufficient health facilities, poor quality education, lower standard of living and so on. They say that India could not provide them good opportunities that they deserved, so they are in a foreign country. When these developed countries failed and there was a threat to the life of these people, they started crying and requesting the government to bring them back to India. And our government had to show how prompt it is working? So we imported Corona in India.

The workers, professionals, soldiers and farmers in the country contributed their level best to the development of India. What was their fault? They were working on their own, helping their family members. The arrival of Corona infected people had brought the problem in their life. Their daily routine was hampered. They were locked where they were. No doubt, the government showed some signs of helping those people by declaring that the accounts of the farmers will be credited by Rs. 2000/-. It was also resolved that three free gas cylinders will be issued to those took the connection under *Ujjwala Yojna*. Also they declared that the *Jan Dhan Accounts* of women will be credited with Rs. 500/- per month for the next three months. The most important decision taken by the government was that the new financial year will start from June instead of April.

I had some questions. What was new in those decisions as crediting the farmers' accounts was a routine process? If women were to be given Rs. 1500/-, why in three instalments? And what will they purchase in Rs. 500/-? Why the financial year was changed? My first reaction was that the financial year 2019-20 will be of fifteen months. It means most of the people will come under the higher tax slabs. I doubted the government wanted to earn more money through tax collection. But after some days, I came to know that I was wrong.

The only decision I liked the most was of issuing three free gas cylinders to *Ujjwala* beneficiaries, because it was directly benefitting the poor and they may not need to go out in search of wood for cooking. I did not understand the issue that if lockdown was for 21 days, why three instalments of Rs. 500/- each. There was perhaps logic of the government behind the declaration of package that declaring help for three months can be shown as a big package. And if the lockdown ends in twenty-one days, the government would not need to spend more on the next two instalments. If the government continues the lockdown, they need not spend more than what they had declared. Hats off to the government of India.

The government of India had started Contributory Pension Scheme for which equal share of the government and the servants are credited to the DCPS or NPS account. The same amount is invested in share market on the recommendations of the experts (?). In the initial stage of war against Corona, the share market fell down and the money invested in share market might have lost. Who will be benefitted with this? Those who are rich will buy shares and own the companies. Who is the beneficiary here? What should one expect from the government at such juncture?

When there was nothing to do, I thought if I had gone to my native place, the situation could have been better. I could have gone in fields. My home is about a kilometre away from the village. Means it's a farmhouse. No doubt, few houses are nearby. But they are at such distance that I might not have been in need to lockdown myself and my family. I could have sat in the veranda for hours together without a fear to get infected by Corona. Even I could have spent enough time in the fields as well working there or just sitting under the dark leaved trees passing the time. But I was unfortunate. I can only imagine what would have done? Due to the temporary common illness of family members, I could not leave my workplace. So I had to lock myself where I was. Complete lockdown. Closed door only to open when we had to go on the terrace. Everyday children were playing there for almost an hour a day. We, the elders, used to just stand on the terrace looking at the garden and the less travelled roads. Again, come back at home. Even we did not open the main gate of the house for two days. I was the only member who could go out to purchase grocery or bring milk. That was only for few minutes; but it was not a daily activity.

Daily quarrels between my son and daughter had become common. My wife had tired of it. Sometimes she used to beat children and sometimes used to cry on her own. One day, I warned both of them to adjust with each other and not to quarrel. Otherwise I would devise new ways to deal with them. But on the very next day, my son came down complaining about his sister. I reminded him of the yesterday's warning. So he left the home and went back on the terrace to play. Within ten minutes, she came down crying and complaining her brother. I then called my son down. Once again I reminded them of yesterday's warning. They were sat in each corner of the bed. I stood in front of them. Suddenly, I slapped both of them and asked them to stand at different places and not move unless I permit. It was a form of punishment.

Generally, I avoid punishing children. I go on explaining how the mistakes of others can be accepted and how our family can be good one. But I was rather strict today. After some time, my son asked for water, but I did not permit. Perhaps it was also a shock for him. But I had to correct them. So I was strict. Then I sent him to drink water. Then he asked for a book to read, perhaps to enjoy the punishment. After half an hour, I left them free warning them that they will not be allowed to play till the end of the lockdown, if they quarrel again. Once I freed them, my son asked his sister to accompany him to play; but she was not ready. After three unsuccessful requests, he went up alone and my daughter took a book in her hand.

5

Lockdown Day-VI, 30th March, 2020. I was eager to go out to purchase the grocery and vegetables. I asked my wife to get ready. We left for the city. At first we had taken the vegetables. Their costs were increased; but you need to purchase vegetables and grocery whatever their purchase cost may be. Then we went to the grocer's shop. Purchased some grocery; but I did not get the sunflower oil, a pack of fifteen litres. So we went home, put the purchased things and went back in the city in search of oil. When we entered the main *chowk*, we found many people commonly traveling on the roads. Some were on the bikes and some on their feet. Piaggio, Tempo, tractor, etc. goods carriers were common on the roads. I was surprised. The people were moving like there was no curfew at all. I said to my wife:

"As the days pass, seriousness ends."
"But, they are not supposed to do so."
"What else they can do?"
"They have to take care of themselves. Otherwise police….."

What the police will do? Though it was the sixth day of lockdown in India, for us in Maharashtra we had been suffering for nine days, right from the '*Janata Curfew.*' For the first few days, people took it seriously. They had well thought of curfew. They thought that the curfew was for them, for their wellbeing. Any limit, any barricades, any compound loses its honour after a considerable period. In the first few days, people did not go out of the house to protect themselves. As the time passed, they had been tired to live in such condition. So they started going out to buy grocery, vegetables, to withdraw money from banks, to visit the doctors for common treatments and so on. So the number visible on road had become the greater one. The police were very strict in first few days. They were beating the people to control them. But then they allowed people for shopping as per the directives of the government. Anyway the number increased. I purchased the goods from the grocer's shop where the long circles were drawn with *rangoli* to maintain the social distancing.

While coming back, I preferred the less travelled road. It went through the market place. I was surprised to see about hundreds of stalls of people selling vegetables and fruits over there. The market was crowded like the usual days. What of maintaining the social distance? There was only one positive thing that people had used masks to avoid the infection. My wife became serious.

"This is dangerous."

"No, this will be common."

"What will happen if went like this?"

"Nothing. The government on 14th April will declare that everybody should join the work. Keep yourself safe. Don't spread the disease. Use masks ….."

"Surprising."

I explained her that people know that shops are open, they are supposed to visit them. If the market was open, we were supposed to be a part of it. And there was nothing wrong. The government had opened the markets in the Metropolitan cities as well. Only the instruction was 'keep distance and stay safe.' It clearly showed that on April 14th, whatever the situation may be, the government will ask the people to join their work. One more thing was there that the wise people if come to know that the Corona was under control and it won't spread as it was expected. The people will think that if they protect themselves with the use of mask, there is no need of lockdown.

The number of Corona positive cases reached up to 1071 in India and 220 in Maharashtra. Out of which 29 people died due to this calamity. Every day, I used to call my sisters and parents. Now there was nothing new to talk except the Corona disease. All my sisters used to tell me the same things again and again. Don't go out. Take care. Like a wise man I used to assure them that there was no chance of infection here.

During that period, some messages used to come on WhatsApp that changed the mood. A message said: 'Just imagine what will happen in next fifteen days. Listen to this audio clip.'

: Hello!

: Hello! How are you?

: I'm fine. How are you there?

: Not bad. But the upcoming days would be troublesome.

: Lockdown is there?

: Yes, lockdown is here; but the situation is worst.

: What will happen? What's the condition?

: Very sad. There is no place for the patients to quarantine.

: Means?

: The number of patients is increasing rapidly.

: But I heard there are only 20 to 25 patients in Mumbai.

: The government do not tell anything. The situation is worst here.

: Then what will happen?

: The patients perhaps will be quarantined on the playgrounds.

: Where do you work in Mumbai?

: In Nagpada Police station. But difficult.

: It means 14th April is not the end of lockdown?

: You can only dream it. It won't happen in reality.

: What about your family? Are you taking proper care?

: Yes, but can't say anything. Because the cases are increasing rapidly. Children and wife have been sent to Solapur.

: When?

: Before the lockdown. It is the satisfaction that they are safe.

: You are alone there?

: No. My parents are with me. I also requested them to go to Solapur; but they said that they would stay with me. My mother told: "Let it happen with us, what happens with you." So they stayed here.

: Take care of them and take care of you.

: God knows what will happen.

: See you, bye.

: Bye.

The other audio was focusing on the situation in Nagpur, Maharashtra.

: Hello!

: What about you?

: Fine. What is the condition in Nagpur?

: Worst. Total down.

: But the media said that only fifteen people are positive?

: There are two hundred cases in all; but the reports from local authorities are negative. Now their samples will be sent to Pune.

: Negative is negative. What difference does it makes in Nagpur or Pune?

: They are the local labs. They don't know the ways of testing.

: What will happen then?

: Total lockdown.

: For how many days?

: At least three months.

: Shocking.

: But real.

: Ok, take care.

: Bye.

This was not enough; but most of the messages focused on the press conference by the Finance Minister, Government of India who declared a package for the next three months. The people used to talk that after 14th April, the government will continue the lockdown for at least one more month. They were perhaps preparing us for the lockdown.

But today's situation in the market showed no sign of lockdown. Everybody was involved in his or her work. No doubt, all of them had masks on their face to avoid the infection of Corona. I thought that as the markets of Mumbai and Pune are opened, the same things will happen in the rural areas. It means, there will be an official end of lockdown on 14th April, 2020 provided that all the people will be asked to take care.

6

31st March, the year end. The news on television said that the new year will start from 1st July, 2020 onwards does not mean that the financial year 2019-20 will continue for three more months. It was a good step taken by the government. It means the fear that was in my mind that the government wants to collect more and more taxes from the public was not right.

One more news spread that was a press note issued by the Superintendent of Police, Satara District which said that the people if found spreading fake news on the verge of 1st April will be punished as per the existing laws and regulations. 1st April is known for 'April fool,' to make fools of others. To deliver fake news and spread the rumours as if they were true. Most of the times, the people used to give the news of someone else's death or accident; but these were all fake news. Sometimes people used to react by just smiling. Then the messenger used to be sad. He used to go somewhere else to cheat others. The person could only satisfy, when he causes somebody to cry or abuse. If the news is given to the old, they don't know about 'April Fool,' they feel frightened.

Anyway, the people won't spread any news because it was lockdown. The government was the controller of the public. They have to issue orders only and we were the ardent followers. One thing interesting happened today. Two days before one of my friend had told me that I could get petrol if I carry my identity. So I just went to the petrol pump. There were almost fifty people who stood with their bikes on the road. There were few policemen who used to enter four people at a time. The latecomers used to go ahead so that they could get the entry in a short while. The police came and warned them to go at the end of the line. One of the bikers said that he was on the right track. It made the policeman angry and he threatened whether he wants to get petrol or not. Then the biker without uttering a single word went to the end of the line. I had entered the petrol pump. The man there asked how much I needed. I asked for the petrol of Rs. 250/-. I took it, paid for it and returned home with a great pleasure. I used to feel if anybody in the family gets ill and there is no petrol, what shall I do? How shall I take him or her to the hospital? But the fear ended and there was only satisfaction.

There was one common advertisement on the television for public awareness. It said, Corona is spreading fast in the world. Our government is trying its level best to fight against the disease; but the people are required to be at home. Complete lockdown. Those who need to go out should use masks for the safety. Always wash your hands with the sanitizer or the soap. Don't spread Corona. Be at home, be safe.

Sometimes, there used to be the images of the policemen, doctors, nurses, workers and the sentences below:

"We are working for you. You cooperate by living at home."

One of the messages received was a story. Meeena is a doctor by profession. She has a two year old son. She loves her husband the most. She was the only daughter to her parents. She loved and obeyed her in-laws, no chance for anybody to complain. Her in-laws also loved her a lot. But today she was very nervous. She was working for the Corona patients. She feared, perhaps, the disease can enter her home only because of her, so she decides to go to stay in the hospital till the end of the disease. She was not aware whether she will come back or not; so the tears rolled down her cheeks. She worried for her son. But there was no alternative available to her. So she called her parents to her home. She collected all the family members. First, she went to the bedroom, kissed her son twice or thrice. Again she cried. She had slept her son and went back to the main hall. She told her husband and other relatives about her plan to stay in the hospital. Further she explained that if she gets infected by Corona virus, nobody would visit her. And if she dies, nobody in the family will go out for her funeral; the government authorities will do that.

Her mother started crying; but her mother-in-law reminded her promise to take care of them till the end of their lives. She also questioned whether she had thought of her son and parents. Everybody was against her except her father-in-law. He was a retired military officer. He was with her. He knew whenever he was to go to join his duty; he was not sure whether he will come back or not. Still his patriotism made it easy for him to join his duty. So he found nothing wrong in Meena's behaviour and said that she was right and everyone should support her decision. So on the next day, everybody helped her to pack up her bag. She kissed her child, touched the feet of her husband, in-laws and parents and said bye to all. There were tears in everybody's eyes. All members asked her to come back home at the earliest. They wished for her work and hoped for the best to happen.

The news of *Markaz Tablighi Jamaat* was in Nizamuddin, Delhi from where one thousand five hundred forty-eight people were taken out. Out of these twenty-four people found Corona positive and four hundred, seventeen people had the same symptoms like Corona and other one thousand one hundred and seven people were quarantined. In this *Jamaat*, the people from sixteen countries have been participated. The people came on 12th or 13th of March, 2020. And today I saw the news where the Chief Minister, Delhi Government wrote to LG, New Delhi to file an FIR against the organizers. Almost all the channels started discussing the issue of Islam and fundamentalism. The Muslims were openly blamed that they are causing harm to India in the name of religion. It was said that people over there spread Corona from Kashmir to Andaman.

Even in my home, my wife said that these people are very bad. All the temples and gurudwaras are closed and what had happened to these people that they had spread the disease. I did not react suddenly. I said I cannot talk like you; but I have to think more. Then I thought, if the people from sixteen countries had participated in this function, then who had issued visas to those people? Why our country did issue visas without medical check-up when the whole world was suffering from Corona. The curfew imposed from time to time where it was told at first not to gather above fifty people at a time which then decreased up to twenty people and finally on the lockdown, nowhere people could gather more than four at a time.

If this was the situation, didn't our authorities know that people have gathered there? Why didn't they close the programme and sent people back to their countries? Or did the government wanted the things to happen? If the organizers are punished or prosecuted, what will be done with the officers and security agencies that were responsible for that? I had not seen the *Markaz*;

but the discussions on the television channels said that the *Markaz* was on the walking distance from the Police Station. Still they had not done anything to disperse those people. Then who was responsible for this situation.

On a television channel the governor of Kerala said that the organizers were responsible and expressed the need to prosecute those people. Moreover, when the anchor asked why those people might have gathered despite the warnings given by the government, the governor said that the people who were mentors from the organizer's side used to say that mosque is the best place where one should die. And that's why the people gathered there. Whoever may have been right, but whatever had happened in Delhi was not right. It is not God who will save you, but you will save yourself from Corona. If you pray or not, it doesn't matter much; it's related to self-satisfaction only; otherwise, any prayer cannot save you from the infection. It only needs to 'stay at home, stay safe.'

Heart-breaking news came from the economic capital of India, Mumbai that fifty-nine people found Corona positive. And it was reported that one hundred twenty-seven people were present in Nizamuddin. So there was a feeling of fear everywhere. The lockdown became stricter than earlier.

We received the press note issued by the District Magistrate focusing that nobody would be allowed to ride even on bicycle in the small lanes. One can imagine what will happen to you if you will use bike or four wheeler.

The government of Maharashtra issued an order to cut down the sixty per cent salary of all Public Representatives including MLAs and MLCs, fifty per cent salary of Class A and B and twenty-five per cent of class C servants. It was, of course, necessary for the state to have reserve fund that can be used anytime in such a painful condition. There was confusion among the employees that the salary is cut down, but the government assured that the salary will not be cut down, but will be given in instalments. While addressing the people of Maharashtra, the Chief Minister said:

> Don't use AC. We are fighting with Corona. Our fight with Corona is in the final stage. Stay at home. I request the doctors not to close the private hospitals.

7

1st April, 2020. Seventh day of lockdown. Today was 'April Fool;' but everywhere there was a realistic discussion of the ghost Corona disease. Everywhere there was a discussion on *Markaz Tablighi Jamaat* held in Nizamuddin. People participated in it had reached their states, but it increased the work of police and administration. Most of the governments requested the people to approach the police or administration so that the essential medical check-ups can be done and if needed the people can be quarantined. Most important thing was to stop the spread of the disease. As twenty-four people in *Jamaat* found Corona positive, it increased the tension of all the Indians. Everybody feared of the increasing number of Corona patients.

Though I was damn sure that the government would not extend the period of lockdown, and the same was declared by the secretary, Home Ministry, Government of India that the government had no intension to extend the period of lockdown. Though the same issue was discussed again and again and feared at the same time what will happen if the period is extended. The lockdown was a confinement for me. Though there were some special facilities available at home, something was missing. The wife used to serve tea twice a day or more times if demanded more. Warm chapatties, fresh meal, new dishes and everything. One more thing there was a chance to be in the company of children. I decided to use this lockdown to teach my son. He never tires when he is playing; but as soon as we ask him to study he used to start quarrel with my daughter or wife. My daughter and wife also expected him to do everything and learn each and everything as and when taught by them. I tried to tell my wife, if he is doing well in elocution, wrestling and acting as well, then you cannot expect him to be number one even in his studies, because he has number of things to pass his time in playing and practice. After all, she was his mother. She could not be contented with the performance of her son. She wanted her son to progress more and more.

When I started teaching him, he took interest in study. One more thing, he feels comfortable to study with me. I generally motivate him the most and insult the less; so he also respects me a lot. He generally avoids quarrel with me. So watching television, taking study of a son, talking with the friends on the current issues regarding Corona and play with children in the evening at least for some time because the regular business. For the first few days of curfew, I was ill; so I could take enough rest as there were holidays. But once I got cured, it became difficult for me to be at home. It was a confinement for me. Sometimes, I used to think of Pandit Nehru, Bhagat Singh, Mahatma Gandhi and all other freedom fighters who had to pass most of the part of their lives in jail and again in the public interest. Living in jail for others! But we had different time. We had been jailed at our own houses for safeguarding ourselves. 'Stay at home, stay safe' was the motto of the time. We were forced to stay at home; but it was difficult to be at home.

There was a strong feeling in mind that the lockdown should not be extended in any case. People should be asked to protect themselves and be at workplace like those who are working in banks, police and revenue. Otherwise, no God can help the human beings. The power of youth, their energy, their force, everything was useless now days. The grocery shops were opened, markets were opened and we the unfortunate jailed at our own homes. Every time, I hoped that the government should order all employees to join their duties from tomorrow.

The people spread over in nineteen states of India from *Markaz Tablighi Jamaat* became a big problem for all Indians. Not only a problem, but the biggest challenge. The question was how many of them had infection of Corona and with how many people they had shared their disease. Then how will it be stopped? And if it won't stop, what will happen to us? The police and administration were tracking those people, used to check them up and if needed, quarantine them. The cases of Corona with the addition of the cases found in Nizamuddin increased the total number of Corona cases. Still, there were some states such as Zharkhand where there was not a single case reported of Corona, but almost all the coroners from Kashmir to Andaman was under tension. Thousands of people were quarantined, hundreds of reports were waiting. If the reports found negative, there was everlasting happiness to the suspected, to the neighbours, family members, villagers, townsmen and all the government officials. Perhaps, this was the only event where people were finding satisfaction in others' satisfaction.

The issue of Nizamuddin *Markaz Tablighi Jamaat* was seen through a different eye. Everyone started blaming Muslims. They are very religious. They have blind faith in Allah. And they consider that death in *masjid* is the best death. The governor, Kerala State, on a news channel told that he had seen the speeches delivered in *Jamaat*, where people were motivated to take active part in religious activity. He also pointed out that when the speeches were going on, many people were coughing. And still the people were not sent to the hospital. It was really a blind belief of those Muslims who participated in the *Jamaat*, though there was a danger to their life. They had neither feared of the government nor their own death. Had they got tied a bandage on their eyes so that they may not see anything from the real world? They only think of life after death. What is the use of that philosophy which does not allow you to live your life in a good way? And why people follow such Gods and their religions as well?

When Corona entered India, the first thing that was closed was the temples, mosques and gurudwaras that means the place of worship was closed. If the Gods are real, why don't they free their believers from the disease? Even no God all over India did revolt against the lockdown. We must remember that we have created Gods, and not the Gods created us. So we have to save ourselves. God is no one to save us; but these people had belief in their God for whom they were ready to die, they were ready to break the law of the land.

About three hundred eighty-six cases increased within a day in India and the tension aroused. There were two groups: the first asked for immediate imprisonment of Mullah Saad, The Chief of the Nizamuddin *Markaz*; and the other group said that only Mullah Saad was not responsible for what had happened. The investigation authorities had closed their eyes and now the *Markaz* is made the scapegoat. In such a time, Media took the side of the government. When I was studying in schools, we were taught that media is the fourth pillar of democracy and it is responsible for the success of democracy; but here media became the slave of the government. So called secular panellists on the television channel said that *Markaz* is an organization which works to spread Islam all over the world. They motivate small children to be the terrorists. This is an anti national and *talibani* organization that it should be banned. Some Muslim leaders who were also present on the news channel tried to refute the charges levelled against Mullah Saad saying that he is not a criminal; he is a religious leader of fifteen Crore Muslims in India. The anchors were trying to trap them in a net by asking as to why he has not surrendered himself to the police.

No doubt, all these people participated in *Markaz* ignored the suggestions given by the governments and did not quarantine the people from abroad as a result of which the Corona was spread. This is not enough, but people from *Markaz* went to various states for religious preaching. And here lied the problem. Many people were infected and despite the lockdown, Corona spread all over India.

I don't know what had happened to the people. Temples were closed, mosques closed, gurudwaras closed; still most of the people found in the mosque who went for *Namaz*. Many times the police beat the people; but they did not stop. Every day, there was a news from one or the other province regarding the punishment to people who gathered in masjid for *Namaz* despite the lockdown. But these were very trivial things. What happened in *Markaz Tablighi Jamaat* in Nizamuddin, Delhi was really shocking? It threatened all the country. In all three hundred twenty people affiliated to *Markaz Tablighi Jamaat* found Corona positive. This was the highest number detected in a single day so far. Apart from these three hundred twenty, sixty-three cases of Corona infection found in India. There were in all three hundred eighty-six cases found in a day.

Those who left *Markaz* went to various states and in various masjids. The tension was how many people had come in their contacts and how many of them might have been infected. The question was when this turmoil will stop? What will be the final number? Even in Maharashtra, we heard the news that one hundred-thirty in Ahmednagar, one hundred eighty-two in Pune, forty-seven in Aurangabad, five each in Satara and Vardha and so many people from other districts had come from Delhi Markaj and it had raised the tension. If these people had been infected, what will happen to others? Whether the Corona will spread more? These were the innumerable questions to which no certain answer was there.

For the first two-three days of lockdown, most of the people were serious. They locked themselves in their houses. But as the days passed, the seriousness went off. And people started going out to see what is happening in the city and not to buy the essential things. This was the reason as to why Corona spread in India. The rate of its spread in India was very meagre, if we compare with China, Italy, Spain, Britain and America; but it did not mean that we need not care. The police had to be very strict; so they used to punish those who come out without valid reasons. It was reported that thirty crimes had been registered and almost two hundred-seventy vehicles have been taken in custody by the police so that it will affect others and they may not come out so that effective social distancing can be maintained. Otherwise what's the use of lockdown? Why the farce of 'Work from home'?

The Chief Minister, Government of Maharashtra, took the issue of lockdown very seriously. He was very concerned about the health of the people; so he warned that he may close the essential services as well if needed. He asked the people to follow the guidelines of lockdown strictly. He and the Health Minister were the real heroes for us. These two people did a lot to control the spread of disease. The Chief Minister had undergone through heart surgery few years ago and advised not to take stress. Still, he was continuously in work only for the people of Maharshtra. The health minister's mother was very serious. She was admitted in the hospital. Still, he was working 24x7 to control the disease; so they were the real heroes for us.

But what happened in Delhi was really shocking. And the Government of India did not stop the *Markaz* and allowed the people to spread the disease all over India. What a sad demise it was? All the states were following lockdown and those people from *Markaz Tablighi Jamaat* reached the disease in every corner of the country. Delhi government was criticised for that; but it is said that the police department in Delhi is under the control of the central government. So the police were working under the Home Ministry, Government of India. The central government, hence, can neither blame Delhi state government nor the *Markaz*; because the foreign people participated in it had come with the permission of central government. I can't understand as to why those people were not tracked by the government when the lockdown was declared. Or did our government have given a free hand to *Markaz* to go and spread the disease anywhere they want?

Today I was very nervous. I thought of my parents living in my native place. A big house in the farm, only two people living there in it. A long veranda in the front of the house and a farm at a distance of hundred metres. There are twenty-five trees of drumstick. The vegetables are grown near it. A very good place to live.

After a month or two, we use to visit our native place. My children also enjoy the atmosphere. When we are in our native, we use to spend most of our time in the field. We do not need television or any other device to entertain ourselves. It is said that the nature makes you forget all your worries; so we prefer to spend most of our time in the field either working or playing in the field.

Every day, I use to receive a phone call from my father. He is a very handsome old man in his seventies. He just uses to ask how about of us. But with the spread of Corona, I was very much concerned about my parents. I told him not to go in the village. When he told me that my mother goes to the village to sell the vegetables, I told her not to go in the village for there was a danger of Corona infection. My mother is a very hard-working woman. Though I am earning and giving them enough money to serve their needs, she works hard and uses to earn money. It is perhaps a self-respect due to which she continued her work; but every day I use to tell her to not to go to sell the vegetables. My parents, every day, watch the news channels; so she knew it better that it was allowed to her as it came under the essential services. She continued her work despite many warnings of infection given to her. Here I was jailed in my rented home at the workplace. Again and again, I wish to be there with my parents in such a time. It was impossible now because of the lockdown. When I used to lie on the mattress, I used to wish to be there.

Here I was without work. Teaching to my children, playing with them and watching television became boring. Whenever I used to switch on the television, I used to find the same news about Corona. There was nothing new except the change in number of Corona affected and dead people due to it. I also feared of Corona infection; but my mother told me:

"If somebody is to die, let it happen. Don't worry."

Only I could do was to think if I had not been ill before lockdown, I would have been with my parents.

8

On 2nd April, 2020; lockdown Day-9. With the spread of Corona due to the programme organized in *Markaz Tablighi Jamaat*, the government of India and all the state governments woke up again and decided to be stricter. Even the Prime Minister talked with the Chief Minister of all the state on teleconferencing. The government of Maharashtra also resolved to follow the lockdown very strictly. Today on every regional channel, we heard the news that the police had become more active and they had taken many vehicles in their custody so that people may stop coming out of their houses and the spread of Corona can be controlled.

We have seen a number of times if the police decide to do anything, they can do; because they have powers. Even in the rural areas we had heard of lockdown that was followed strictly. Somewhere the police use to beat people severely. Somewhere they punished them by letting them Yoga on the road. Some police used to request the public not to come on the road. Anyway, whenever there is riot or curfew, only police have to maintain the law and order. When all the people live at home with the family members, police have to say 'good bye' to their family members; so we have to respect them.

But what happened in Bijnor, Rampur, Dharavi, Gaya and Indore was really shocking. When the news spread all over India that the people from *Markaz* had been reached in all the corners of the country, the police in all the states were asked to find out those Muslims and forcibly quarantine them; and the symptoms of Corona found visible, admit them in the hospital for the further treatment. But in Bijnor and Gaya, the people revolt against the police and start throwing stones at them. Then the government of Bihar handed over this job to Anti-Terrorist Squad. What a great tragedy? The police who hurl their life in danger for the well-being of all the citizens are troubled without any reason.

Today was the festival of 'Ramnavami', the day of the birth of God 'Ram'. Every year it is celebrated all over India enthusiastically; but today the people forget Ram. This was a good step taken by the people and government as well. If people might have gathered on this occasion, there could have spread of Corona. In Indore, when the doctors went for the medical check-up, the people spit on the doctors. Now days, the God was manifested through the doctors, police and few good government employees who were fighting against Corona.

Any government gets a credit of a good work done; but the central government seems very much greedy for getting the credit. In India, there is National Relief Fund. It is in force from 1948 when the then Prime Minister Pandit Jawaharlal Nehru; but the present Prime Minister Narendra Modi had changed it as PM CARES FUND for which he must be criticised, but no event of dislike was shown.

For the next three days, the government of Maharashtra had decided to strictly follow the lockdown; and it was visible. I did not listen the sounds of bikes or vehicles. Even the grocer's shops were closed. No vegetable shops and nothing else. Only twelve days have to pass. If government makes it stricter than earlier, it doesn't matter; but the period of lockdown should not be extended.

One thing positive happened. It was a good thing that the World Health Organization had praised India for controlling the spread of Corona when Italy, Spain, Britain, America and all the developed countries have knelt themselves and are quite sure that they can't save their people. In Italy it is said that if a person above the age of sixty found Corona positive, he is left to die; he is not treated. They only treat the patients below the age of sixty. Even the American President Donald Trump also guessed that one lakh and fifty thousand people may lose their lives in America. Generally, people used to say about India that here we have poor health facilities, no safe water to drink, low quality education and uncleanliness is everywhere; but as a true Indian I felt proud when people who had gone abroad for education or employment were very eager to come back. 'East or West, India is the best.' I thought that if Nizamuddin *Markaz* incident had not happen, the number of Corona positive people might have been restricted around one thousand.

9

Lockdown day-10 dated 3rd April, 2020; my head was aching. I could not sleep last night as well. The news that was spread on the television channels had increased the heartbeats. Everywhere there was a rein of fear and terror. There was a complaint received which said that the Corona patients from *Markaz* misbehaved with the nurses. And some started questioning the treatment given to women in Muslim community. Some started talking on domestic violence, polygamy, *talak* and many other things. No doubt, everywhere you may go, you will find the mixture of good and bad people. Some are good, some are better and few are the best at one side; likewise, some are bad, some are worse and rest are the worst. Like a world, India is a good mixture of people where we talk about unity in diversity. Different states, different languages, different dresses, different castes, different religions, different cultures; still, there is something which had bound all the people with the feeling of brotherhood. The news that was being spread by television channels targeted the Muslims for being fundamentalists, for going in mosque for *namaz* again and again despite prohibition by the law. The people who participated in Markaj and those who spread the disease in every corner of the country must be criticised. Everybody will agree; but the media should keep in mind that it should not result in the conflict in society.

There was only positive comment by one of the ministers; government of Maharashtra who said that the news against the Muslims was being spread without any reason. When he was asked as to why the Special Forces were deployed in Muslim areas so that the lockdown can be observed, he said that not in Muslim area but the areas with dense population should be saved from the infection; so the government had taken a decision. It has nothing to do with the Muslims. On the question that the people came from foreign countries were found in the mosques in Mumbra, Thane; he said that they had come to India with the permission of government of India. They had to go back; but due to lockdown they could not go to their home country as a result of which they had to live in the mosques. The news on media was that there were Bangladeshi Muslims found in those mosques who had come without permission; so the Muslims in the area were considered anti-national. Thank God, the responsible person from the government confessed that the people living in mosques were not only Bangladeshi; but they were the citizens of different countries.

Today, our Prime Minister while addressing the citizens thanked them for their support to the government in the time of lockdown. He said that we are fighting with a common enemy. This disease had challenged the mankind, the whole world is afraid of this disease. Every nation in the world is looking at India with a feeling of surprise, so we are sure of our victory. He further reminded us about the '*Taali Bajao, Thaali Bajao or Ghanti Bajao*' that was held on 22nd March, 2020 and asked the Indians to give nine minutes at 9.00 p.m. on Sunday, 5th April, 2020. He directed the Indians to switch of the lights and go in the balconies or look out through the windows with candles, lamps, batteries, torches, mobiles and see the power of light which will inspire us to fight against Corona.

This was again a new event. Our Prime Minister is event lover. He loves organizing events. In all he is a good event manager. Every time he is in search of events. Thank God, he had learnt from what had happened on 22nd March, 2020. People had forgot the social distancing and came on the roads in groups with drums in their hands and still we were proud of its success. Way to a new event. Generally, the opposition parties do not dare to counter the Prime Minister because he is very good at changing the words and bringing sympathy to him. In Gujarat election, it was the feeling that Congress party will win the election. And one of the leader while criticising said that Narendra Modi's politics is lower class; but he changed it and said that the opposition named him for being a low caste. While addressing the people in a rally, he asked: 'Is it an offence to be a low caste person'? And the election took a turn.

Moreover, he is also known all over the world as anti-Muslim due to the Godhra riots. In the same election in a rally, he said that the Prime Minister of Pakistan had told the Congress to make a Muslim the Chief Minister of Gujarat. He further asked a question to the people whether they will accept the Chief Minister sent by Pakistan. It turned the match and BJP won the election with a slight majority. So the opposition leaders do not dare to talk against him. But today, even the ministers from the state government criticised him and questioned the wisdom in organizing such events when people were dying and infected of Corona. Again there was a hidden fear that people may come out of their homes to celebrate the event forgetting the principle of social distancing. The Corona had given at least some strength to the opposition.

The number of Corona positive people crossed two thousand; still we were enjoying because the rate of Corona spread was meagre, if compared to America, Italy, Spain and Britain. The developed countries had knelt before Corona; but China could come out of it at the earliest. It was said that China had created the virus to trouble the super power. What a great surprise? There was Corona infection in Wuhan in China; but it did not reach Beijing. Here in India, it spread from Kashmir to Kanyakumari and Rajasthan to the North East; but China had controlled it. No doubt, they had closed down Wuhan for few weeks; but sent Corona in almost two hundred countries. Italy, Britain, Spain, Americas and other countries were reportedly said that they have good health facilities, accepted their defeat openly. There was a statement from Italy that they could not save their life. Even the American President said that the next fifteen days would be very dangerous for America and controlling Corona was not possible. The Prime Minister, the Health Minister and even the King of Britain were infected due to Corona. It means Britain also knelt down before Corona.

Talk with anybody; he was not sure whether the lockdown will end exactly on 14th April. If it, it's ok. But if no, how long will it be extended? In a meeting with the Chief Ministers, the Prime Minister had talked about devising the ways to control the infection even after closing lockdown. But today, the government of Punjab said that if Corona is not controlled, the period of lockdown can be extended. Even the medical experts, Indian and abroad as well opined that there is real danger after the end of lockdown.

10

I was born in a village, the only son to my father. My mother had given birth to four daughters; then I came on the earth. Even after my birth, my mother wanted one more son. Unfortunately, she gave birth to one more daughter. Then the cycle was ended. Total lockdown; no more children to come out again.

Indian culture made my parents to give birth to six children. They wanted a son who can continue their name. At least half of the purpose of their life had become successful when I was born. Now they had to be ready to fight against the fate. Only two acres of land, drought prone area, many children to feed. So my father used to work in fields of others. He was a regular worker. Producing children is an easy task, but feeding them the most difficult. My mother was in charge of everything. She had to work in field, cook for the children, and milk the cows and so on.

The children of the poor are also hard working. My four elder sisters started helping my mother when they grew up. It was a diffcrent time when the girls were not sent to the school; but my parents had progressive thoughts. They send all of us to school. I became twelve years old. Then I had to go to the planes to graze the cattle when I used to come back from school. I was good in study; so my mother dreamt that I shall join any government service. I was really impressed by my teacher. So I wanted to be a teacher. I used to tell my mother that after twelfth, I shall take Diploma in Education; and then I will be a school teacher. Unfortunately, I could not get admission to Diploma in education. I joined, then, undergraduate college. Then I thought to take admission for Bachelor of Education so that I could join secondary school as a teacher. I took admission to post graduate college and there was a turn to my life. I started reading the literature of Phule and Ambedkar. I was very fond of God; but as the years passed, I went away and away from the God.

11

On 4th April, 2020; eleventh day of lockdown, my wife received a message and she came to me. I was lying on the mattress, tired of long jail at home. My twelve year old daughter, requested me to at least let her come with me out of the home; because she was also tired. A girl of twelve, how long could she study? She is good in study. If I or my wife accompany her in her study or tell her to do on her own, she continues her study for hours together. She was studying grammar, Maths and all other necessary subjects that she need to know to face competitive examinations. From last year, she had started enjoying reading literature, especially non-fiction. See how the fate changes the way of your life? She was so clever and hard working girl that everybody, not only the family members but also her teachers and class mates were sure that she will qualify the State Scholarship Examination or may get admission to Jawahar Navoday Vidyalaya; but neither she admission to JNV nor she could qualify the scholarship examination. Last year, she had participated in elocution competition. She started her speech with confidence. She was the first participant who could get loud applause from the audience as a result of which she got feared and forgot everything and could not finish the given time. At that time, she decided that she would never participate in elocution competition.

My son, good in elocution and wrestling as well at the age of eight, won many trophies. When my daughter knew her result, she cried and asked as to why she could not succeed despite of hard work done in last two years. When she thought of her brother's success, she said he had not worked that much harder as compared to her and still he was the winner in the eyes of all. I tried to console her; but she declared that she will take part in the Elocution Competition and definitely win it. And here it all started. She became successful this time. She had achieved the mastery in speaking that when she starts speaking, her body speaks, her eyes speak, her face speaks and everything in all conveys her message with force to the audience. What else the speaker needs?

We generally say that there can be a speaker in ten thousand; but I am fortunate enough to have two speakers at home. So the situation had changed at home. People generally say that there is loss of communication among the family members; but we talk a lot at home. Each and every news was discussed at home; so my children read books, mostly the biographies. When human beings start reading books, his thinking capacity increases and a person with good logical reasoning do not accept the views of others as it is. They think over it again and again. During the period of lockdown, we had many discussions at home over the spread of Corona and the steps taken by the governments to control Corona. Whenever I called others, the people on the other end used to say that they are tired of controlling their children. My case was different. Whenever I'm free, my children want me to talk with them. I listen to my children; so they listen to me. It was visible on their faces that they want to go out, but they did not do it. One day my daughter asked me for a ride over a bike; but when I told her about the danger, she took her words back.

One day I asked them to draw pictures. My daughter drew a picture of a girl who was helping a small boy in his study and other girl was watching with surprise. It was a beautiful picture. But what my son drew was really surprising. The picture was entitled as 'Corona.' There was a home near which a boy was smiling as he was safe from Corona because of following social distance. Next to it was a road on which the funeral procession was going on and only few people were present. I became happy to know that my son is very mature in his small age.

Today I received a message. It said that in *Shiv Puran*, there is a reference to Corona; and there is a 'Shiv Coronashtakam' to protect oneself from Corona. The same was even shown on the television channels. Many priests tried to justify how it will be beneficial to protect the people from Corona infection very confidently.

I was looking at the things happening all around in India. I could see only through the television channels. *Markaz* was on the target. Everybody criticised *Markaz*; even the Muslims requested their community members not to go to mosques for namaz. Some feared that the issue may be transformed into conflict between Hindus and Muslims. A firebrand political leader said that the people in *Markaz* should be shot dead.

The videos that were viral had contributed a lot for the defamation of Muslims in India. One video consisted of three youngsters out of which two had masks on their face and they asked the third where he was going. He replied that he was going for *Namaz*. The former two people beware him of Corona; but he put on his cap over his head and told them that 'if you believe in Allah, no Corona will touch you.

The other video showed that all the Muslims collected in *Masjid* for *Namaz* were sneezing continuously only to spread Corona. Another video showed that the young Muslims were talking with each other; and the topic of discussion was Corona. One of the young boys said:

Corona is a proof sent by Allah. You were asking for the proof for NRC and NPR. You said those who won't be able to provide the documents will have to leave this country. Now, Allah will decide who will live and who will go.

Other video showed that the people were spitting on the food, but they were just airing the food which was their tradition; but it was shown that those Muslims were spreading Corona.

At the same time, some people from media checked whether the videos were real or fake. And I found few links which told that most of the videos were created in foreign countries and there was no relation of it to the Indian Muslims. The video of spitting on food was explained in a different way. There is a *Bohra* community which has special Mosques and they do not allow even Sunni Muslims over there. They do not spit on the food; but they air it and then start eating their food. It means the video was not related to the spread of Corona; but it was a religious activity.

The Chief Minister, Government of Maharashtra said very strictly that no such message should be viral on social media; otherwise, he will save Maharashtra from Corona ; but nobody can save oneself from law. The criminals will be prosecuted. He requested all to cooperate the government. At the same time, he suggested that if needed, the period of lockdown can be extended. He warned to not to organize any religious programmes.

The social workers also contributed a lot in those days. They had provided masks and sanitizers to the needy. The vegetable shops were open, the grocers shops were open, hospitals were open; but the people who need not come out used to come on the road. Some people were found on the road for the evening walk. Some people go in the parks. It was reported that most of the people were found on the terrace ignoring the social distancing; so in Pune, the police had issued the notices to the Housing Societies and warned that the officials of the societies will be responsible if the people break the rules of lockdown.

12

5th April, 2020 was the 12th day of lockdown. It was a special day. Three days before the Prime Minister of India while addressing the nation requested the citizens to give nine minutes at 9.00 p.m. that day. He wanted all the citizens to switch off the lights and lighten the candles, lamps, torches or mobile flashlight as a symbol of victory over the Corona. Like a 'Prakashparv,' he had imagined of the event. All the TV channels tried their level best to motivate all the Indians to be a part of this event. The number of Corona infected people had reached up to three thousand. But a new drama was to be staged that day. Those who will oppose or not participate in it will be taken as anti-national. Most of the TV channels said the citizens to take part in *Prakashparv* to show the world that all the Indians are fighting together against Corona. They also repeated that '*Taali Bajao, Thaali Bajao, Ghanti Bajao*' was a great success and it was praised by the world; so spare nine minutes at 9.00 p.m. today to show our unity to the world.

Most of the WhatsApp groups were active. Some were in favour of *Prakashparv* and some were against it. One video message I found which was shared by a nomad. He said:

..... do you think that we are rascals. Do you see the word 'silly' written on our foreheads? We expected you to talk on Corona, the steps taken by you to control the spread of Corona. We expected you to declare package for the farmers whose milk is unsold, the vegetables are spoiled and thrown out of the fields. We expected the package for the workers. We expected you to talk on whether you will definitely end the lockdown. We had expected you will declare some policy about the workers who are walking for hundreds of miles without having food to eat. But what did you say? 'Taali Bajao, Thaali Bajao, Ghanti Bajao.' And now light the lamps. What kind of lamps you had lighten in last six years. If you had done it, you would not have asked us to light the lamps. Our decision is final. Final means final. We won't switch off the lights and lighten the lamps. Final.

From the Prime Minister of India, he had expected the right things. In last six years, the country had a great set back. In 2014, I remember, Narendra Modi had criticised the then Prime Minister for the weakening of Indian Rupee from Rs. 54/- to Rs. 57/- per dollar. Now, the Indian Rupee had no value at all; it had been weakened to Rs. 74/-. Now nobody talks about it. Media had closed its eyes six years before. Whenever they talk about Modi, they praise him. They had blind themselves. A gas cylinder that we used to get in Rs. 335/- and still the Congress lead government was criticised of corruption. Today, we spend Rs. 700/- or more for the same cylinder; but the king is pure like washed rice. Many times the *Bharatiya Janata Party* agitated against the increasing prices of Petrol and Diesel; but we used to get Petrol for Rs. 50/- to Rs. 60/- per litre though the cost in international market was at its height. What is the present situation? Today the oil prices in the international market are at the bottom; still we are paying Rs. 80/- or above. Then the question arises what we had received in the last six years. The answer is nothing. Our present Prime Minister is the best speaker in the world and that speaking ability and not the development of India had reinstated him once again as the prime Minister of India. He had befooled us. He said there was corruption in the reign of the Congress party; but today there is no corruption, the subsidy is directly credited into the beneficiary account. I have been thinking for the last five years; if there is no corruption, the prices should come down. But the prices are continuously rising. I can't understand yet what kind of corruption Congress had done by providing the things at reasonable rates.

I received the first page of a local newspaper which explained the fact that on 5th April, 2020; the *Bharatiya Janata Party* has completed its forty years; so the same day had been chosen by Narendra Modi. It means the lamps all over India are to be lightened to celebrate the forty successful years of BJP. It has nothing to do with Corona. People have closed all the temples, some have stopped going in mosques, and the churches are locked. They had stopped celebrating the festivals and *jatras*; and the Prime Minister is celebrating forty years of success of his party. And most of the people will follow him like silly people by switching off the lights and lighting the lamps or torch.

Some people were of the opinion that the lights of the lamps or candles will create energy that will help to defeat Corona. He might have consulted with those clever astrologers. Lighting a lamp, for some people, was a humble duty. They thought that they were supporting the Prime Minister by lighting the lamps. If the Prime Minister spreads the superstitions in the country, what else do we expect from such a country?

Many people told me that the lockdown will be extended; but I was constantly of the opinion that till 14th April, 2020; there will be near about five thousand cases of Corona infection. Even the people who will be in contact with those five thousand will be quarantined and the lockdown will be ended. At least like bank, police or other essential services employees, the people would be allowed to join their duties carrying a valid identity proofs. Till date, I was fortunate enough that there were only three cases of Corona infection in our district. So I assured myself that the lockdown will end on 14th April, 2020.

When the Science or its knowledge is not enough, the person turns towards the religion. Look at the tragedy. The temples and all other places of worship were closed and the government started two TV serials – '*Ramayana*' and '*Mahabharata*.' This was the first year in the history of five hundred years, when the Ramnavami was not celebrated in India. This was the favourable time for India and its people to know that the Gods are useless and the Gods can manifest only through the doctors, nurses and police. This was the first time in the history of India to know that science is superior to the religion. There was a chance to transform Indians from religion to science; but what a tragedy of our country! The Prime Minister is asking the people to light the lamps so that we may win the fight against Corona. There was also news that the Chief Minister, Government of Uttar Pradesh, had a dialogue with three hundred seventy-seven religious priests asking them to follow the lock down.

In a discussion on a television, one of the panellist said that they were ready to light the lamps, but let the Prime Minister talk about the health facilities. "How will he further deal with this issue"? He asked. The spokesperson of Bihar and Delhi state governments were of the opinion that despite their demands of masks and ventilators, the Central Government did not provide these things. Still, they will light the lamps as per the guidelines given by the Prime Minister. A famous Yoga Guru came forward and requested the people to support the Prime Minister. When he was asked how the lighting the lamps will help in stopping the

Corona infection. He told that 'lamp' symbolises 'a bright future.' It will show the entire world that all Indians are united in the fight against Corona. It will enhance the confidence of the Corona warriors. They will think that all the people were with them. It showed that there was conflicts among the Indians-few are in favour of lightening the lamp and few against it.

13

My wife already declared her decision that she would not participate in the Modi event. I was also of the same opinion. At 5.00 p.m., my daughter told me that my son had said our neighbour that we were going to light the lamps on the terrace. I respect the views of even my children. So I asked my daughter to charge the mobile. I was busy in watching the news and wife in cooking. During this time, my son and daughter had produced a play. My son was the director of the play. Both the children took part in the play.

At 9.00 p.m. I was not happy to follow them on the terrace; but to respect their views, I went to the terrace. My wife also followed us. My son lit the candle. My daughter switch on the flashlight of the mobile phone. Lights were switched off. It was the twelfth moon. Those who were living on the ground floor came out of their houses. All of them lit lamps everywhere, some turned on the flashlights of their cell phones, and some had their torches to move around. At one side my daughter saw a big *mashaal* and asked how they had prepared it. I told her that the old clothes are wrapped around a piece of wood having iron at the top. It is then wet with oil and is lit to get enough light when one is in darkness.

The nine minutes passed. The candle lit by my son got dissolved and we thought of going downstairs; but my son expressed his sorrow. He said that they had prepared a play and they were supposed to present in front of us; but my daughter lost her interest and said let's go down to watch television. But my son caught hold of her and said that they have to present the play urgently. Then the play started.

My daughter was the narrator today. She narrated the purpose behind the presentation of play. She said that their aim was to spread awareness among the public regarding Corona. My son and daughter came on the stage. There was no such stage; but the terrace was the stage. No drapery. Simply presentation only. The two friends started talking that they are going to a party. One of them rejected the offer on the ground of Corona; but the other friend took the former by force to party. They started coughing and sneezing. My wife became very sensitive. It means she could not see her children being infected even in a play. She got angry with the children and asked them to stop; but being curious to know what will happen next? I stopped my wife and asked our children to continue.

Their roles were changed now. My daughter became the police; so she stood with a small stick in her hand. My son seemed to go in the city just to wander despite the lockdown. My daughter stopped him and asked as to why he had come out. He just kept quiet. Then she asked.

> "Don't you know the curfew is going on? Do you know about lock down? Why did you come out? You people had spread the disease. You are the criminals of society."

My son was silent without uttering a single word. Then she beat him with a cane in her hand. He said sorry. Then she asked him to jump like frogs as a punishment. The last scene was very impressive. Both of them took hold of each other's hands and declared their decision to defeat Corona by helping each other.

When we came downstairs of our home, I thought that at least today's event resulted in the children's creativity. Then we switched on the television where there were news all about the *Prakashparv*, lighting the lamp. I saw one interesting tagline: '9 Minutes Diwali will Defeat Corona.' Many politicians, celebrities and common people also took active part in this event. Media as usual gave it the best coverage; so it became a grand event.

The cases of Corona were increasing rapidly. It had crossed three thousand and five hundred out of which one thousand cases was the result of *Markaz*. If we exclude the cases caused by *Markaz*, the cases were two thousand five hundred. It means still the disease was under control. Due to lockdown, the cases of Corona did not increase. Other news I received on WhatsApp that said that the Minister, Higher and Technical Education will meet all the Vice Chancellors through teleconferencing to take the decision regarding the university examinations. I wished that the government should declare well in advance as to when will end the lockdown.

14

On 6th April, 2020; the 13th Day of lockdown, I got up early in the morning with the end of a dream. I was at my native place. There were three containment zones at the village; so those areas were locked. In the first place, five people found Corona positive; in the second, four and eight cases were found in the third. The police were very strict. I was on the bike. I was going to water the crops; so I was on the bike. Soon I saw my father in the village. Actually, he was supposed to stay at home; but I didn't know as to why he was there to break the rules of government. My father is a very simple man. I was surprised to see him.

Where are you going, Anna?
Home.

He had a wooden stick in his hand to support himself. He seemed very tired. Why did he go to the village? If he needed something, he could have asked me to bring it, I thought. Without thinking much, I told him that I shall leave him at home on bike. He said, 'Ok.' When he was sitting on my bike; I got up and came to know that it was not real, I was in a dream.

It was not the tiredness of my father who was tired of living at home, it was my tiredness and it was my children's tiredness.

All the citizens were tired of living at home; so I had the dream. Whenever I listened to the news regarding the extension of lockdown, my heartbeats would increase. I feared and wished again and again that it should not be extended.

My wife might have been tired of lockdown; but she did not show it. Whenever the children express their wish to go on the road outside, it was she to oppose them. I used to tell her to excuse them and allow them to go out when there is nobody present on the road. I thought it won't violate the rules. Being a mother, she had to protect her children; so she had to be so strict and that she did well.

The tiredness due to lockdown took me back to the medieval period in the history of India. There are many stories of *Mughal* emperors who had their *zananas* where they used to keep their wives. As the wife was considered the *izzat* or the family, she was not allowed to talk with any other males in the family. She was used to meet only male who was her husband. As there were hundreds of women in zenana, they had to wait for years together. Sometimes, if the king likes any girl, he used to bring her by force and keep in *zanana*. He used to enjoy her sexually to satisfy himself. Afterwards, if he likes the other, he used to avoid the former. But she had to live in her own cell in the company of other maid servants or *hijras* who were kept for the security of the wives of the emperor. Only their sons could meet them as and when they wish. Imagine what would happen to us just by imagining to get ourselves locked for a lifetime? Only the imagination created fear in my heart and mind as well.

This system was not prevalent in Muslims only; but the *Rajput* and the other *Kshatriya* castes also followed the same pattern. Their women were always kept in their cells. They could not know what is happening outside their cell. And if they could understand about the outside world, they could through their maid-servants only. There was no difference for them between the day and night. Closed doors, closed windows and closed eyes. Everywhere there was darkness. Darkness outside and the darkness inside. How might have they lived inside the room?

Ok. At least, due to the lockdown we had understood the plight of those women right from *'Ramayana'* and *'Mahabharata.'* The richer the family, the grief of the women was greater. The women from the poor families had to struggle a lot to earn for their living expenses; but they were allowed to go out of the house. They could meet anyone. There was no such barrier for them; they could talk with other males without any restriction. The reason was not that the poor people were considerate for their women; but they had no alternative available without work.

Good news received that day. The educational minister declared that as per the guidelines received by the central government, the examinations will be organized in three sessions a day. The results will be declared as soon as possible. One thing was clear that the university examinations will not be cancelled on any ground. There were rumours and even the students used to call us to ask whether the university examinations will be cancelled due to the lockdown. The minister made it very clear that whenever the lockdown ends and whatever the conditions there may be; but there will be examinations. He also explained that the masks will be compulsory for all students at the time of examination. He added that the principle of social distancing will be followed strictly. It was a clear message for all the students, teachers and other stakeholders.

The doctor in our local area shared an audio message on WhatsApp group that I received in the evening. It was really shocking. He said that he had checked a thirty year old female patient who had a dry and the severe pains in her throat. He asked about her travel history. He came to know that she had not been to any foreign country; neither had she come in contact with any Corona patient; but the doctor became sure that he was suffering from Corona; so he had handed over a letter to them which was addressed to Chief Medical Officer of the Rural Hospital in our city. The patient and her relatives reached at 10.00 a.m. with a letter in their hand. It was Saturday, a half day for the doctors. When the relatives of a patient shown a letter to the officials in the hospital, they were answered that the Medical Officers won't be available due to Saturday; so they were asked to go back. The patient and her relatives went back to the doctor who was the narrator in the audio message. He then called the Symboisis Institute for it was told on the TV channels to inform so and so if found such and such symptoms. Unfortunately, the doctor was not entertained for half an hour. Then one of the doctors available over there talked with the narrator. He inquired about the history of the patient. At last, he asked the narrator to give a letter to the patient addressing the Chief Medical Officer, District Civil Hospital so that she will be admitted there and further treatment can be done. Then he did the same; so the patient and her relatives went to the Civil Hospital; but the patient was not entertained at all. The two lady doctors very reluctantly said that the cough and cold patients if sent over here, how shall we manage it here? They did not even touch the patient and sent them back by giving them some medicines.

      The narrator did not know what had happened to the patient on Saturday and Sunday. The patient was known to the narrator. On Monday, he sent a young boy to see what had happened to the patient. The boy came with a reply that the patient had come to his hospital and waiting out of his OPD. When the patient came in OPD, he was told that they were not entertained in Civil Hospital. Then the narrator asked the patient as to why she had not come on Saturday in the hospital. The patient told that they were so tortured in this process that they did not wish to come back to the hospital.

Then the narrator admitted the patient in his hospital. He also told that he had registered a complaint to the local authority regarding the carelessness of the government officials.

At last he said that the things that are told on television, radio and newspapers to contact so and so if found such case is false. The government officials are not very serious about Corona. Perhaps, he feared that there could have been twice or thrice cases in reality than the numbers are reported in media. If you find the patient suffering, support him, admit him and start the treatment. Don't let him or her send to the government authorities. They are not taking proper action. If this is the situation, why to report the cases to the government, when they are not taking it seriously. If that patient is Corona positive, I thought that Corona was in the yard of my home. Till date, I thought there is no chance of infection because there were no Corona positive cases in all sides within twenty kilometres. My confidence was no more today. I lost my confidence totally.

It was my guess that the rural life will not be affected by Corona. People will continue their work without disruption and still there will be no danger to their life. But it was my guess. Guesses are just guesses; they need not be true every times. A taxi-driver working in Mumbai had come to his village, Nisare on 22nd March, 2020; and yesterday he found positive. We used to believe that if within fourteen days, the person does not show any symptoms, he can end his home quarantine period; but this patient did not show any sign even after fourteen days. So nobody could resist his contact for everybody was sure that he is not positive.

We think in one way; but things happen otherwise. He had come in contact with at least seven hundred people. Then how long those seven hundred had gone. God only know it. When he was found positive, at first the swabs of the family members were taken. His brother and daughter's tests were found positive. The village was sealed. Nobody was allowed to go out, and nobody to enter in the village. Now the whole village was quarantined. The administration had wake up and started investigating deeper and deeper so that the chain of infection could be broken. It means a taxi-driver was an alive-bomber who without any limit wandered everywhere in the village, talked to everybody, only the God knows how many people had been infected.

The number of Corona infected people was increasing rapidly. The other news received. When we were studying in schools and want to write an essay on science for example, we used to write the first sentence: 'This is the age of Science.' Only the topic used to change; but the rest of the sentence was same. So now for me, it was an age of WhatsApp, Facebook and Twitter. The true and false as well, the news reach lakhs of people within a minute. The news was that a sixty-three year old Corona positive woman dead in a neighbouring district whose travel history told that she had been to Satara for two days and six days in a village in our tehsil in the period of lockdown. When she suffered from cold, flew and coughs, she was admitted in the hospital. For two days, she took the treatment in a private hospital. But then she was shifted in the government hospital, where it was detected that she was Corona positive. Her travel history again hurled one village in danger. The government of Maharashtra very kindly had taken the decision that the work in farms need not be stopped; just take the basic precautions; so the farmers were working in field without any tension. The village was at the feet of the fort Chandan-Vandan, totally away from the urban life. The people over there might have been very confident that there will be no danger for them. But this had brought a calamity over the whole village. The total village was sealed by the government. It was also decided to test all the people in the village. Everything was beyond imagination.

The most critical and worrying news came that the Wockhardt Hospital and Jaslok Hospital, Mumbai were sealed. It was found that the doctors and nurses working in these hospitals found Corona positive. Those who were in the hospitals were not allowed to go out. It was decided that all the patients, nurses and doctors' swabs will be sent to the lab and then Corona positive people will be quarantined. If the nurses or doctors were not safe, what would happen to the common and poor people? Now I came to know as to why the nurses had agitated against the Bombay Municipal Corporation, Mumbai. They said that they were ready to work; but give them personal protection equipment (PPE Kit). Their safety should be definitely a matter of concern for the government. When those two hospitals were sealed, one can imagine how many people would be found positive. If the people in the two hospitals will find positive, how many people had come in the contact with those people? What will happen?

This was not enough; but 'Matoshri,' the residence of the Chief Minister, the government of Maharashtra had become Corona hotspot. So the security guards of the Chief Minister had to undergo medical check-up and if they are found positive, the security staff might be changed. These were all the possibilities. One thing was very sure that *MarkazTablighi Jamaat* had spread the disease all over the country. Due to their contact with the foreign people who came to participate in Markaz, they became the Corona carriers. They travelled from Delhi to all corners of the country by train; so there was a big problem to find who came in contact of those carriers and whether they had been Corona positive. Is this a never-ending problem?

15

There were four people in a small city named Islampur who went to Hajj to worship Allah. Unfortunately, they carried Corona in their body and brought it to India. India was not lockdown then. The airport authorities had done the thermal check-up of these people. They had no fever. Still, as per the guidelines of Government of India, the airport authorities stamped on their hands which said: Proud to be quarantine at home.' They were orally told to quarantine themselves at home for fourteen days. They went to the Railway Station by a taxi. Then by train they arrived at Karad station from where they reached home through taxi.

When they reached home, they forgot what they were told at the airport. As they entered the house, their children and grandchildren came to them. They also enjoyed a lot. Up to this point, they had not even got fever; so they became sure that they need not fear of Corona. Their fear had decreased and the confidence took place of fear; so they thought that they do not need to quarantine themselves.

We Indians are very naive. If he a person returns from religious pilgrimage, the whole village comes to his house to touch his feet. By teaching his feet, they think that they will get the punya as equal to the person who had come from the *Tirth*. The Muslims are not different from us. Many relatives had come to meet them. They whole-heartedly express their satisfaction and organized a grand party which their daughters and other close relatives had attended. In all, there were eighty people. All of them enjoyed a lot. They had eaten a *biryani*. They cut three big goats for the party. On the next day, the guests went away.

All the four people started their regular life as nothing had happened to them. They started their regular work. Going to market, bringing the grocery, going for a morning walk, joining mosque for *namaz* and so on. Then the Prime Minister declared a '*Janata Curfew*' to be observed on 22nd March, 2020. Before the end of '*Janata Curfew*,' the Government of Maharashtra declared the lockdown for three days. Then the central government increased the lockdown up to 14th April, 2020. Meantime, all the four Hajj travellers suffered from severe cough cold and high fever. When they were admitted to the hospital, they were shifted to the Civil Hospital. The doctor asked about their travel history. Knowing that they had come from Arab countries, immediately they were quarantined in the isolation wards. On the next day, the samples of their swabs were sent to Pune. The news reached the whole city that all the four *Hajj* returned people were suspected to be Corona positive. Everybody was talking about their contacts and feared that Corona might have been reached in the whole city. Everybody was eager to know the reports of those four patients.

On the next day, all the four people were found Corona positive. The government took the necessary steps and started searching the people who came in contact with those people. The city was locked from outside. All the roads coming to the city were blocked by barricading it. Immediately, the family members and the people in contact were asked to undergo quarantine. Within two-three days the cycle became visible. Every day one or two people showed the symptoms of Corona. In the neighbouring district where there was not a single case reported, yet the first case was found. It was a lady who was the daughter of one of the four infected patients. The city atmosphere was full of fear. The number of Corona infection went on increasing from 4, 5, 7, 9, 12, 13, 22, 24 and finally to 26. Every time the government used to find the history of the patients and were meditating over to whom one has spread the Corona. To find the people in contact with the Corona positive person and ask them to quarantine had become a regular business. In this process, half of the city was quarantined at their homes. Everywhere the roads were quiet. No traffic; almost all the shops were closed. The people were not allowed to go out of their homes without permission. To break the cycle of Corona infection, the Central Reserved Police Force was deployed in and out of the city. People were also told that if they take care, they will be saved. Only message was given to everybody, 'Stay home and stay safe.'

Everybody in the city blamed those four people for violating the rules of the government which had brought misery to the whole city. I felt that these people should be charged by National Security Act for hurling the lives of the citizens in danger.

16

When the entire world was trying its level best to protect against Corona, India was involved in bringing the students and employees of the industrialists who were trapped in the foreign countries. They had been brought to India by the special aeroplanes. If they had been checked as and when they were landed in our country, there may not have the need of lockdown. At least, the government should have raised the quarantine centres; and those who came from abroad if asked to quarantine there for fourteen days by force; the Corona might not have spread in India. But those rich people came to India and became the Corona carriers spread the disease in the whole country with both their hands. It means because of those rich, the poor people in the country were left to suffer.

The *Tablighi Jamaat* was criticised a lot on the ground that it carried Corona all over India; but nobody was ready to talk on who had given them the permission to organize the event. If the government of India were alert, they might have either sent back the foreigners from the airport or they might have been quarantined so that those who had carried Corona with them might have been sent back.

It is generally said that there is no value of poor people. What were their crimes who were working for the well-being of the mother earth? Why did the people get more importance to those who had left the mother earth and those who continuously abused our country and spread the rumours all over the world that India is poor and dirty nation where the standard of living is very low? Those who were loyal to the mother earth had to undergo a severe punishment; their jobs were taken away and they're jailed in their own homes. The poor were left to die. Most of them while going to their native places on their feet without food to eat and water to drink. Nobody helped them. No doubt, some non-government organizations came ahead with ration and all other help. But about twenty-nine people died when they were on their way to home. The fast trucks had dashed them and their lives end. What was their fault? If they had been informed in February or earlier in March, they might have managed on their own without the help of government. But they were left to die. Some state governments also provided food and shelter to those who lost their jobs. Some police officers also provided meal to the beggars in the city.

The only question torturing every minute to me was when the lockdown will end. Today, the Maharashtra Public Service Commission postponed the competitive examinations to be held on 26th April, 2020. The Corona cases were increasing day after day. One more news on a Business News Channel which said that the lockdown will end from June to September in certain stages. If one case is found, the same place becomes the containment zone of Corona. At least, two-three more cases are found because the infected person spreads his infection to his family members. What happened in one village in our district was that the Corona infected person's daughter and brother found positive. This was the use of lockdown. If you don't come in contact with your neighbours, there is no possibility of infection from either side. So everybody was advised to stay at home to stay safe.

17

A new case was reported in Nashik which had become a new containment zone of Corona. The government tried to identify such hotspots, so that they can be sealed to stop the spread of the disease. There were five such zones in Mumbai as well; so the areas were sealed. One unpleasant thing happened in Dharavi, the biggest slum in Asia. When the first patient was pointed out, the administration became alert and they imposed curfew in the area; but the young boys over there threw stones at the police saying that the lockdown was not for them. I thought as to why those young boys had thrown stones at the police who were trying to save the lives of people by hurling their lives in danger. Then I thought if ten people live in a single room, how can we expect the young boys to be in the house for whole day and night? If out of ten, four or five are women or girls, they can manage themselves at their homes. How can one expect such things?

There was sixth patient found in Satara district in a very small village named Mharugadewadi. A man, who was found Corona positive, was working in Nerul, Mumbai. He was a rickshaw driver. He was driving rickshaw to earn his living. During the period of lockdown, he had come to his village by his rickshaw. There were no Corona symptoms visible in him; so he freely moved from here to there in the nearby villages. He had come in contact with almost thirty-five people along with two private doctors. He became ill, but he had not thought that he was suffering from Corona. He took it lightly. He met two doctors. Though they asked him to take rest at home, he moved like a free bird from one village to the other. He had been on holiday; so he went everywhere he could go. But when he was admitted in the government hospital, his swab was sent to the lab and was found Corona positive.

Now the whole village was under tension. The whole village was sealed. Those who moved freely in all the corners of the village; now locked themselves at homes by closing the doors. Every mother was serious. Nobody allowed their children to go out. Everybody was feared of infection outside. Despite the government's requests and warnings, the people were so confident that they won't be infected by the disease for their village is away from the main city; but it was their mistake. The person who was Corona positive like a live bomb wandered all over the village. Everybody was looking at others with suspicion of having Corona infection.

Those who had passed time with this rickshaw driver or had a talk with him went in *coma*. They had thought that perhaps their life had come to an end. They locked themselves in the separate rooms. They wished to meet their children or grandchildren for the last time; but they had no courage to open the door. They feared that any wrong step can bring disaster to the family. Even the family members changed their behaviour. The women in the family used to cook and knock the door to hand over the meal. They were not allowed in the kitchen for lunch or dinner. Even the people in the village tried to maintain the distance even at their own homes. Most of them blamed themselves for not keeping social distance during the lockdown. If they had followed the lockdown, there may not have been any danger. Those, who did not come in contact with the rickshaw driver, thought of themselves as fortunate. Those who lived in the fields and had not been to village in the last four days were happy; because they were sure that there was no danger for them.

The government authorities sealed the village. At first, they tried to know his travel history. There were at least thirty-five people and two doctors he came in contact with. The police shifted his family members in the isolation wards in the first stage. Now they turned their attention to those who came in contact with the diseased. Again the same questions were asked to them regarding their contacts. All the thirty-seven people were put in the isolation wards and their family members were asked to quarantine themselves at home. The whole village was closed in their rooms. Social distancing was changed to family distancing; because everybody was under pressure.

The government had banned the social gatherings; so the Markaj was criticised. But it was not the only case. The ruling party MLA in Karnataka Mahantesh Kavatagimath arranged a marriage ceremony of his daughter in the presence of three thousand people among whom one was the Chief Minister, Government of Karnataka; among the other were the Ministers of the state and central government and the political leaders of all parties. There were also two banners giving information of Corona infection. No social distancing, only celebration was there. When the people in power break the rules; even the media closed its eyes. Only one or two newspapers talked about it.

In Maharashtra also two politicians were charged for they worshipped the God *Vitthal* despite the lockdown. If the influential people break the rule, the common people feel that they should not take it seriously. So most of the people broke the rules of lockdown and the police had to take action against them. Some

Muslims criticised those events not because they were serious about the lockdown; but because *Tablighi Jamaat* was criticised.

Today on 8th April, 2020; what happened on a television channel was somewhat different. A spokesperson of MIM asked the anchor of a news channel that if the one thousand and five hundred out of five thousand Corona patients belong to *Tablighi Jamaat*; then give the details of who are the rest three thousand and five hundred. Whether they are Hindus, Muslims, Christians, Parsi, Jain or Bouddha? But the news channel anchor and the BJP spokesperson consciously avoided the discussion over the topic. MIM spokesperson told that out of those three thousand and five hundred, two thousand and five hundred people belong to *Rashtriya Swayamsevak Sangh* and one thousand people belong to BJP. Maybe he was not true completely; but it had changed the whole narrative of the discussion. As usual he was not given enough space and the issue remained unanswered.

I called one of my friends to know what had happened to the sealed village. The work and even the working conditions in the villages are different. The people start their day with the crowing of a cock. Sweeping the yard and cleaning the cowshed, milking cows and buffaloes, etc. works are almost finished before having tea. After that the men in the family go to the dairy to sell the milk. Then few people go to the plains to graze their cattle, few people go to the fields to work. The old people stay at home to look after the children. And if the village is locked down, what might have happened there? I was curious to know. My friend told me that only those people who must do their work go out in the plains or fields; otherwise, all other people feared a lot; so they had locked themselves totally in their houses. Even the government authorities were alert. They had given suggestions to the villagers. The police had not closed their eyes. Even a single mistake can increase the number of Corona positive cases.

There was a discussion on the government level regarding the end of the lockdown; because the government had locked down till 14th April, 2020 only. But as it was the last week, it became a matter of concern whether the lockdown will continue or will it be ended? If it ends, there was a danger of community transmission. Then the very objective behind the lockdown will be killed. If it is to end on 14th, what was the use of the lockdown for twenty-one days. There was other possibility that the lockdown will the continued for the next two weeks, or these areas that are not affected by Corona will be released from lockdown. Due to lockdown, the condition of workers became worst. They depended upon the mercy of the government and few non-government organizations. Even the Cabinet Minister, Higher and technical Education, while discussing with the Vice chancellors told that the university examinations can be started from 15th May, 2020 irrespective of the continuation or discontinuation of Lockdown.

Still, India was in the second phase. It means there was no community transmission yet. Only those people who had the foreign travel history or those who came in close contact with Corona infected people found Corona positive. The Chief Minister of Maharashtra and the Health Minister were happy with their performance, but they wanted to break the complete chain of infection. Till the number of things to be done. The administration in our city decided that only the milk dairies will be open in the morning and evening. In the afternoon, from 12 p.m. to 3 p.m. the grocery shops and vegetable shops will remain open. The weekly market on Monday and Thursday had been closed till the new notification. Only the medicals and hospitals were open all day. Also the authorities after consulting with few social workers and public representatives decided that there will be a police check post at the entry points to save people from infection.

18

9th April onwards, the new guidelines came into force. Though the grocery and vegetable shops remained open for three hours a day; and milk shops in the morning and evening, the medical shops and hospitals were open whole day. Apart from the specified period, if anybody comes out on the road, he was to be punished. The rule and guidelines were constantly changing. As the Corona spreads the more, the rules became more and more strict. And the rules are made for the safety of people.

Today the 'Bhilwara Pattern' was discussed on the television. In Bhilwara, the number of cases went on increasing. And the number reached up to twenty-seven. The Chief Minister, Government of Rajasthan, took the appropriate steps to control the disease. He discussed the issue with the administrative and police officers. He told that the rules need to be followed very strictly; otherwise, it would be difficult for them to control the disease. A comprehensive plan was prepared. It was declared a containment zone and it was locked. Nobody was allowed to enter in and nobody to go out. The people in the area were told that nobody will be allowed to go out of their homes. The people were forced to be at home. The Corona suspected cases were quarantined. As Corona is a contagious disease, it spreads from one person to another; so it was needed to break the chain of Corona spread. Though by force, the people stayed at home, the chain of Corona was stopped completely. It is said that one can infect almost three hundred people in a month and the chain continues further. The administrative and police officers tried their level best and successfully broken the chain of infection. Still, the chief Minister stated sadly: "The two out of twenty-seven lost their lives." But he was proud to say that all other twenty-five patients became Corona negative after continuous treatment. And no new case of infection was found there. He was also praised by the news channels. The police on duty then paraded on roads to celebrate the victory where the people welcomed the police by showering the flowers.

Baramati, a newly developing city in Pune district, where I took my education, was in the process of becoming the epicentre of Corona. A vegetable vendor was found Corona positive and the turmoil started there. There was a danger that he might have spread the infection in all over the city. At least two hundred people might be coming to him a day. How many people in all might have been infected by him? It can be discussed later. At first, the government authorities took his family in their custody and their swabs were given for the check-up. His daughter and brother found positive in the first stage. Then the police and the health assistants started surveying the entire city by visiting every house and asking whether any person in the family had visited the vegetable vendor. Those people who told that they had visited the vegetable shop, the first advice was given to them to quarantine themselves. They were warned to follow family distancing; otherwise there was a danger of infection to the family members as well.

In all six people found Corona positive who were shifted to the hospital. Hundreds of people were quarantined at their homes. Still, the people in the city were coming out to purchase the essential things. The danger was visible. If the chain is not broken, the whole city may be at stake, so the administration and police thought that 'Bhilwara Pattern' be implemented in Baramati. Let nobody to go out. Hotspots to be finalized. Hotels to be transformed into isolation wards where the Corona suspected people can be quarantined. So seal the borders, search the cases, point out the hotspots, quarantine the people and break the chain of Corona had become the daily business.

Heart-touching news attracted my attention. A nurse was working in the hospital where the Corona patients were served; so she had decided not to go home so that the infection may not reach at her home. She had a two years old daughter. She was very concerned about her daughter; but she thought that there was a danger coming home every day. Maybe she will bring the infection with her and the family members will have to suffer. All her friends had decided not to go home so that at least the family members will be safe.

As her daughter was two years old, she with her father went on the fourth day to visit her. She came out of the hospital. Her daughter and her husband wearing the masks went to visit her. When she saw her daughter, the tears rolled down her cheeks. She wanted to embrace her daughter; but the nurse in her stopped her from doing so. She just smiled at her daughter. Her daughter got down the bicycle. She was to go to her mother; but her father said:

"Don't go to your Mom. She's in the hospital."
"I want to meet her."
"Just see your Mom from distance."
"Why"?
"To avoid infection."

Then the small girl kept her aback. Smiled at her mother and again sat on the bicycle. Then she said good bye. Afterwards, the small girl and her father went back home.

The good news came. Those Corona affected found positive in the initial stage, now their treatment was completed and they were sent to their home. Still, there was a danger of infection; so the cured people were asked to quarantine themselves at their home.

Dharavi was such a slum where in a ten by ten rooms, fifteen people used to live. So to quarantine the people in Dharavi, the schools were taken over by the government. The health minister further said that one toilet is used by four hundred people. So, even the toilets were sanitized.

All over the country, everywhere there was a talk on Corona; but the people were not serious. Shocking news came in Maharashtra. It had made the people to think whether the rules are there for the rich or not. It was reported that DHFL's Badhawan family had been to Mahabaleshwar from Khandala with twenty-three people on a trip; and he had got the special permission from the Chief Secretary during the lockdown. The Home Minister, Government of Maharashtra, expressed his regret over the issue. The opposition party attacked the government. If the news were true, it was a corruption. In the lockdown, the movements of people had been stopped. Many times it was advised to be where you are; and what we find here is the person who is responsible for the implementation of the decisions taken by the government is violating the rules. Very sad.

There was one lady doctor in Delhi who was talking to her husband on the video calling. Last seven days she had not gone to her home. The government had provided the facility to the doctors and nurses to live in the hotel to avoid the danger of Corona infection to their families. They had enough food to it. The hotel workers and all the officials used to welcome the medical staff in the hotel by clapping for them. They were proud of themselves. But who is not afraid of death? Everybody wants to live. I feel that those who commit suicide are the most courageous people. What courage is required while getting killed oneself? People kill themselves in many ways; some by taking poison, some by hanging themselves, some by shooting themselves, some by jumping down from the terrace of the six-seven storey building, some by burning themselves and many more ways. While committing suicide, they do not think of anyone; if unfortunately they get severely injured and do not die, they suffer a lot, they beg for their life. They ask their relatives to save them.

The medical staffs have to perform a double duty to cure the infected patients without infecting their own family members. Their own life was uncertain because there were many cases reported so far of the doctors and nurses who were found Corona positive while serving the patients, they had got their own life at risk. They could not do anything to save themselves instead of taking proper care by using masks and sanitizing themselves. The problem was, we as a country, could not provide them personal protecting equipment (PPE) kits. They worked by using raincoats which was not so safe. They had no option but to fight against Corona.

To save their family members, those people who had stopped going home; always there was a fear whether anybody of them will get infected. We had seen the people who served in the armed forces and live without their family members most of the time. Some of them get the quarters; but others can meet their wives and children only when they are on holidays. When they are on duty, only audio or video call is the medium through which they can connect their family members; but now all the Corona warriors had been living the life of soldiers. Their enemy is no one but Corona.

There I watched different news on the television where the police officer had sat in front of his own bungalow. He had come to meet his family members; but he could not dare to enter his home for he feared of infection. He knows that his life was in danger; but he did not want to hurl his family in danger. He sat out of the gate of his bungalow on a boulder. And called his family members at the gate. His wife and children were happy to see him. He talked with his children from distance. He asked them to take care. When his wife asked them to take care. When his wife came with tea in her hand, he was confused.

"Stop."
"I've brought tea for you."
"It wasn't needed."
"But you're at home. I can't send you like this."
"Wait."

He went away and told his wife to put the tea outside the house. She did it and went back to the gate. Then he picked up a cup of tea and started drinking while talking with his family. He also wanted to embrace his children; but Corona has prohibited everything to him. Then I thought that I was fortunate enough to be with my family. No need of distancing; only to spend time with the wife and children. Here I could save my family by keeping myself at home and he could save his family by keeping himself out of his house. He was serving the country by keeping himself out of his home and I was serving by keeping myself at home.

One more news came which filled my heart with enthusiasm; because the school teachers were appointed in one of the districts in Maharashtra to seal the district borders. Now they had become Corona warriors. They had masks on their face and stood on the borders of the district to protect the people from Corona. There was no any positive case in that district. If the infected people are not allowed to enter in the district, all the people will be saved. I also thought to be a part of such system.

In Delhi, the teachers had been given the work to distribute the rice and wheat. Even the Chief Minister praised their work. He said that it is not the work for the teachers; but they are doing it happily. The schools were transformed into the quarantine centres. Our district had only six cases till then; so we were not needed to go out to work. We were just helping the nation by staying at home.

All the states have pointed out the containment zones and the areas were locked. Total lockdown. Only the medical facilities were available. If anybody needs the grocery, they received it at home just on a single call. In the dense population, the hotels and schools were transformed into the quarantine centres. The people who came in contact with the Corona positive people were quarantined to control the spread of the disease; and it was needed. How can the people quarantine themselves where fifteen people are living in a single room of 100 sq. ft?

The lockdown was to end on 14th April, 2020; but the government of Odisha extended the lockdown till 30th April, 2020 and wrote to the central government to stop the trains and aeroplanes; otherwise there was no use of extending the lockdown. Even the Maharashtra government was thinking on extending the period of lockdown. One thing was sure, the newly pointed out containment zones had been locked for fourteen days; it means though the lockdown ends on 14th, these areas will be locked even after the end of lockdown. Many state governments were of the opinion that the lockdown may end in certain stages. There were around four hundred districts where no case was found positive.

Most of the patients were cured till then. They were sent back to their homes. In Islampur, District-Sangli twenty-two patients out of twenty-six became Corona negative. It was the success of the administration and police that they locked the area and Corona did not spread in the city. It was an oasis in the desert.

The active cases were only four now. It had created a ray of hope that the number will down to zero.

19

On the 11th April, there was a celebration of Mahatma Jotirao Phule birth anniversary. We know very well what had happened in Markaj. Almost all the organizations in Maharashtra had decided to celebrate Mahatma Jotirao Phule birth anniversary on 11th April and Dr. Babasaheb Ambedkar birth anniversary on 14th April at home by lighting a lamp and reading a book at home. In the morning, I got up early; but I had to take my wife to the hospital. She had been suffering from cough. There was no possibility of Corona; but the fear over powered her mind. So she asked me to take her to the hospital.

When we went to the hospital, the main door was closed. About ten to twenty people were present. We asked who the last patient was. There was a woman; we told her that our turn is after her. After waiting for twenty minutes, the main door of the hospital was opened. To maintain the social distancing, only one patient at a time was allowed in the hospital. All other patients had placed themselves so that they can maintain specific distance. My wife also took a suitable place. I would not be allowed in the hospital; so I told my wife that till you complete your medical check-up, I shall walk on the empty square road in MIDC. I enjoyed walking on the road for half an hour. I had this opportunity by chance.

From the last month, I had not had this opportunity. No morning walk, no evening walk.

As we came back home, we started the preparations for the celebrations of the birth anniversary. There was no photo frame of Mahatma Jotirao Phule ; so I put a book having the photo of Mahatma Phule on the cover page on a chair. The photo of Savitribai Phule and Dr. Babasaheb Ambedkar were placed on either side of the chair. I lit the lamp. My wife took the photographs of me and my son. Then we started reading the book *Slavery*. It was decided that everybody in the family will read the book in turns.

As there were only four days left to end the lockdown, the Prime Minister organized a video conference of the Chief Ministers to take a review of lockdown. The governments of Odisha and Punjab had already taken their decision to extend the lockdown up to 30th April; but the nationwide decision had not taken yet. So there was a curiosity to know how long the lockdown will be extended. As there was celebration of Mahtma Phule birth anniversary, the reading of a book was going on. So we did not watch the news. In the evening, the Chief Minister, Government of Maharashtra, addressed the state.

> *Thank you very much for your support in fight against Corona. Maharashtra had been a guiding spirit for India and the world as well. While talking with the Prime minister, I told him that Maharashtra will be locked till the April end. I am talking to you to avoid confusion or spread of news based on the guesses. As Mumbai is the gateway of India, the people all over the world if they want to come to India, they come to Mumbai. And then they go wherever they want to go; so the cases of Corona positive are more. We not only want to control the infection but to end the infection. Keep aside the politics. There is a whole life to*

do it. Now it's time to cooperate. You take care, I shall take the responsibility. We shall win a battle against Corona.

He said that the nature of lockdown will be conveyed to the public soon. How the university examinations will be conducted will be cleared soon. He also told that the work in farms was not banned at all. If in some areas, the lockdown is to be released, clear guidelines will be issued.

We received the news that the death rate of Corona positive in Pune was around thirteen per cent. In all, twenty-seven people died out of which fourteen were male and thirteen were female. Many of them were suffering from diabetes or heart related problems. The workers of Municipality had started a survey on home to home basis, so that the infected people could be pointed out and they could get the proper treatment.

When my wife told the doctor that she was suffering from cough, she was asked to sit on the chair in the adjoining room. He did not check her in the usual OPD. At first, he asked about her travel history. He registered her name and mobile number in a register. In the afternoon, the person from the District Health Department called us to know whether my wife was feeling better. It assured us how alert the district government was!

20

It was 12th April, 2020. The end of lockdown was coming near and near. Still two days to go. 14th April was the last day; but the discussion had already started of increasing the period of lockdown. Till that day, Odisha, Punjab, Maharashtra and Bihar had already declared the lockdown up to 30th April. Delhi chief Minister also tweeted that the nationwide lockdown need to be extended.

Some people were of the opinion that as there were four hundred districts in India, where not a single case of Corona infection was found; these districts would be given some concession in the upcoming lockdown. No doubt, the boundaries of the district must be sealed as before; but the people must be allowed to start their work. The Haryana government told that there will be three zones- red, orange and green. For orange and green zones some concessions in lockdown can be given. At least, some industries should be started. In Maharashtra also, they had prepared three zones.

> Red Zone: Mumbai, Pune, Thane, Palgarh, Raigarh, Sangli, Aurangabad and Nagpur

Orange Zone: Ahmadnagar, Satara, Beed, Osmanabad, Jalgaon, Kolhapur, Ratnagiri, Sindhudurg, Nashik, Jalna, Hingoli, Latur, Amaravati, Akola, Yavatmal, Buldhana, Washim, Gondiya

Green Zone: Solapur, Dhule, Nanded, Nandurbar, Parbhani, Vardha, Chandrapur, Bhandara and Gadchiroli

Red zone consists of the districts where more than 25 cases of corona positive people were found. Orange zone consisted of those districts where less than 25 but greater than 15 cases were found and the Green zone consisted of those districts where number of positive cases found so far was below 15.

The former Chief Minister of Madhya Pradesh while criticizing the government said that when he was the Chief Minister of Madhya Pradesh, he had taken some initiatives. The schools and colleges were closed.

Now Madhya Pradesh is going through a very critical condition; because the government of Madhya Pradesh is fighting with Corona without Home Minister and Health Minister. If there are no ministers, how would you fight against Corona.

He was very critical of the central government for they were waiting for the fall of his government. He told a story that on 8th March, twenty-two MLAs went to Bangalore who had not returned yet. The legislative assembly was adjourned till 25th March, 2020 on the ground of Corona infection. But the central government did not declare the lockdown, until he resigned. Consciously, they took the decision of lockdown late which resulted in the spread of Corona. It means to come in power in Madhya Pradesh, the central government left people to die.

One more message received on WhatsApp was very interesting. It was about the political situation in Britain. It is said that time gives answer to everyone. . In 1920, the British Rule was here in India and the Indians were fighting for the freedom. At that time, the then Prime Minister of England, Winston Churchill had said that Indians are not worthy to rule the country. After hundred years, in 2020, the Prime Minister of England, the Health Minister and the King Prince Wales were found Corona positive and they had to quarantine themselves. Then who were governing their country? The answer was the Home Secretary Priti Patel and the Finance Minister Rishi Sunak. Both are the Indians by Origin. Those Indians who were considered unworthy to reign before hundred years had to take the responsibility to run the country of Englishmen. The advice below was: Don't be proud of who you are in present, the future can be somewhat unexpected.

21

14th April is the birth anniversary of Dr. Babasaheb Ambedkar. Already we had prepared ourselves to celebrate the birth anniversary at home only. There was curiosity. We tried to decorate the home. I placed a table closely touched to the wall. Then the photo frame was placed in the centre on the table. I put the 'Indian Constitution' in front of the photo. Then my family members read the book about the principles of Buddhism.

Many artists, philosophers, thinkers and writers had decided to celebrate the birth anniversary of Dr. Babasaheb Ambedkar digitally. Many of them were live on Facebook, YouTube and other social media. The people had attended the programme online. Some delivered lectures, some sang the songs and some drew pictures. Everybody was using his or her talent to celebrate the birth anniversary. And the reason was very simple; the people could not go on without celebration.

Dr. B. R. Ambedkar was the father to all workers, the father to all *dalits*, the father to all *shudras*, the father to all *ati-shudras*, the father to all women, the father to all *adivasies*, the father of all social and economic backward castes and all others.

He had written such a constitution which had given the right to vote to all irrespective of sex, caste, religion and age.

The Prime Minister addressed the nation. Everybody was just guessing what he will say; but nobody can predict what was in his mind. We expected him to give some relief at least to the orange or green zone; but without giving any relief, he continued the lockdown up to 3rd May. He only gave the hint that after 20th April, 2020, some relief can be given by the state governments on a conditional basis only to the orange and green zone.

In the afternoon, it was seen in Bandra, Mumbai; where thousands of people came on the road. The people wanted to go to their homes. They wanted to go to their states. They complained that they do not get enough food to it. The police had to use their force to disperse the crowd. A very sad picture. The entire nation was fighting against Corona and here thousands of people were gathered on the road ignoring social distancing. Then the question arises why those people had come on the road? How did they come in groups? Who had motivated them to do so?

The TV channel said that the police had registered one hundred and ninety-seven FIRs and about thirty-seven people were sent to jail. Some people said that they had come to know through WhatsApp that the people will be sent to other states through ten buses. So they had gathered there. It was declared by the Indian Railway that the money against the cancellation of thirty-nine lakh tickets will be refunded. It means they had booked the tickets. How can this be a fault of people? When thought over the issue, I came to know that the railway administration had given the suggestions to all their employees to be present at the place of work, which clearly gave the message that the railway service will be started. Then the leader of opposition said that the government failed to provide food to these people; so they came on the road. It was the failure of the government. The state government said that the central government should do the needful to send those people to their homes. Even in the deaths of people, there was politics.

People had stayed where they were; because they had hoped that the Prime Minister won't extend the lockdown and they will be sent to their villages safely. When they heard him today on the television, their anger knew no bounds and they came on the road. Thank God, the state government had stopped them. It was said that Vinay Dubey, a President of Uttar Bharatiya Mahapanchayat, an NGO; who considered himself as the leader of North Indians was arrested by the police for sending the wrong message on WhatsApp as a result of which this mishap took place. Even the correspondent of a television channel was arrested for showing the news under the heading: 'North Indians will be sent by 100 buses'? Only the state government was criticized by the news channels.

Most of the people said that Modi had extended the lockdown up to 3rd May; because he had to show the public that he had done something different. The Chief Ministers of Odisha, Punjab, Maharashtra and Bihar had extended the lockdown up to 30th April. So he might have done it. Then the question arises why didn't he declare the extension of lockdown first? Was he waiting for others to declare it? The central government finally said that the air and railway transport will not be opened before 3rd May, 2020. And the whole nation was drowned in darkness, that is, Lockdown-2.

Section II

1

During the lockdown the sugar factories were not closed. This had done because it might have caused a loss to those farmers who cultivate the sugarcane. To cut this sugarcane many groups of workers get the contract signed with various sugar factories spread all over Maharashtra. If the factories had been locked, the workers had to live away from their home without work. Secondly, if the production is less, there is a danger of hike in sugar prices. Many workers working in the sugar factories are working either on daily wages or on the contract basis. So it was beneficial for all that the factories were not closed. Also the government had not stopped any kind of work in the field. It means all the works watering the field, growing new crops, harvesting and preparing the land for the new crops. So the sugar factories were not closed.

The sugarcane cutting workers celebrate their Diwali at their native place and leave for the factories to join where they had signed the contract. There is a group of 20 to 50 workers who sign a contract. Their chief is called *Mukadam* who is assigned the work to take any decision necessary for the group. He talks with the sugar factories or the agents. He had some special rights. The farmers also deal with only the *Mukadam*.

Anybody can ask why the workers migrate. Why don't they work in their own villages? Why do they need to live away from their native place? It is a routine for this people. Only old people and school- going children live in the native place. All the workers along with their working force at home, their cattle and Bullock carts come to the workplace. At first they set up their huts made up of wood sticks and the dry leaves of sugarcane that is sometimes covered with the plastic cover. Some people who do not have people at home to take care of their school-going children either admit their children in the government residential schools or they attend the school only for the first semester every year. In latter cases, the children take care of their small brothers and sisters when their parents are out for work. They do not attend the schools. It definitely becomes clear that they take place of their parents while caring the young ones or assist their parents in work which decides the line of their future and fate as well.

These people start their daily routine in the dawn. When men clean the place where the cattle are kept in the evening, the women cook meal for the day. They reach the fields before the sun rise. They cut the sugarcane and fill the bullock cart. All the family members sit on the top of the bullock cart. This is a very difficult task given to the bullocks to carry the cart to the factory. When the cart is filled fully with sugar cane, The Wheels of the cart get deeper and deeper in the soil and it becomes difficult for the bullocks to pull the cart. With the development of technology, now a day the tractors are used to pull the bullock cart out of the fields. Once the cart is brought on the road the bullocks manage it smoothly; but once the cart reaches where there is slope the bullocks have to walk ahead pushing back the cart. In the opposite situation, they have to try their level best to pull the loaded cart. It becomes very difficult for the bullocks to cross that much space. The bullock cart driver continuously goes on beating the bullocks with the whip-cord in his hands.

The money earned in those five six months is used as a annual income. These people mostly take loans from the private money lenders who charge more interest on the amount taken as loan to spend money mainly in the marriages of their daughters. These people spend much money in marriages. The dowry system is the curse to those people living in Marathwada. They take loans for one time, spend it one time in a daughter's marriage and take them almost 10 years to return the loan. If any worker has two-three daughters, he needs to spend all his whole life to be free from the loan he had taken from the money lenders. With the end of sugarcane, the factories were shut down and those people were locked at their work places. And they wanted to go back to their home. There was nothing to be done in the factory area. Then the question of letting these people to reach their home came ahead. Even the ministers of the state government and MLAs of Ahmednagar and Marathwada asked the government to take positive decision in case of sugarcane cutting workers. The government gave its nod to send those workers to their home district. The government also ordered that the workers will be allowed to travel inter district provided that have to undergo medical check-up.

Once the medical check-up is completed, the workers were allowed to go to their home districts. They became very happy and went back to their villages; but the people in the villages had been afraid of Corona infection. So they did not allow those people to enter the village. The people who very happily went back to their home districts became very sad as they were not allowed in the village. They were said to live two kilometers away from the village in the fields. Again they had to prepare the huts in the fields and had to live there. Their own village did not allow them to enter in it. What will be their mentality? They belong to nowhere. When they go to work in sugarcane area, they are known as *Nagari* means the backward people living in the drought prone area. And now their own village when disallowed them to live in their own house, it means their own village also doesn't belong to them. What a tragedy of their life is?

The huts were prepared, and the daily routine started. But they have nothing left with them. And the villagers did not allow them in the stores, market or the banks. This was a new problem faced by those people. They had enough amounts in the bank account but they were not allowed to it. How would those families continue their living without a grocery? Local government officials found no time to look at these people. And the media had closed its eyes. Who will talk on the grief of those workers?

When in the morning we take tea, we must think of the workers who had cut the sugarcane and carried it up to the factories to be processed. And then we have the sugar to add in tea. But the same workers who had done their best in the production of sugar were living without sugar. But there was no one to express their grief. Everybody, common people, social media, print media and TV channels talked about the condition of Corona spread in the cities and the suffering of the people who live in the cities. Many people who help the needy handover all their help to the people in the City; but those poor people had not received help from anywhere. Nobody helped them, neither people nor the government and the God was nowhere.

2

To stop the spread of corona virus the government closed all schools and colleges. A man working in IT sector can work from home. In the same way the government directed the schools and colleges to continue their work from home. Students were given the holidays but to continue their education through online learning was started.

The enthusiastic and techno-savvy teachers prepared the videos to teach some topics to the students. The students had to click on the link through which the video was shared or the e-books on communication skills, grammar, reading skills and also the books on Children's Literature. Many of them contained the online tests. Some were animated texts that the students were supposed watch carefully. The purpose of animated text was to make the learning interesting. Creation of self-videos was the task done by very few teachers. For other teachers, teaching online means to forward the links on the WhatsApp group they had received from the senior education officers.

Let it be. The students had nothing to do at home. How long they can watch TV? How long can they play with sister or brother? How long can they play with their parents? How long the parents tolerate their children? Then what should these children do? How should they pass their time? They are not allowed to go out to play with other children which is their fundamental right. But we need to save the children, so they should be locked inside the home. What will they do then? Either play games on mobile or quarrel with the family members. There is also a chance that they may be psychologically disturbed. So this was the best solution by the government to learn from home. 'Learn from home,' a good name. The students at least spend one or two hours a day. It might serve as a relief to the parents as well.

But in some places despite the lockdown and prohibition to children's going out in the houses of the neighboring children though disallowed, many times in the rural area the children used to come together, play, dance and sing the songs. One thing was clear in the initial stage that they had no chance of getting infected from Corona. It shows that their parents were also careless in the rural areas. Now almost all children became familiar with the online learning. Look at the parody. More than 50% of families in India are using manual cell phones on which internet facility is not available. They have no smart phones. How could they help their children to learn online? What about the rural area where the internet has no speed at all? What about those poor who do not afford 3G or 4G plans of cell phone companies? What did the government thought of those children? Online learning, we can think of in either cities or in English medium schools. How many people are there who have enough economic resources who send their children to the Vernacular schools or government funded schools? Some people keep their children in the Government schools for they will get midday meals. Educationists all over the world say from the root off the navel that the education that you receive through mother tongue is the best education. Sad to say, in India English medium schools have been preferred despite their low quality education, lack of teacher eligibility and its poor output. Even the illiterate people want their children to study in convent schools. They will take loan to admit their children to the convent schools. But if you could consider that the education in mother tongue is the best one, there is no chance that you will admit your children in such schools. How many people are there who admit their children in the government primary schools? These schools were the best one, but the teachers were given non-academic work and the teachers now do not find enough time for which they are paid. It doesn't mean that nobody sends the children in Vernacular schools to enable their children to learn the things through the mother tongue or to get their children developed physically, psychologically and mentally. We cannot ignore this.

Now a day very few people want their children to be in

sports, cultural, social work, elocutions, writing essays, drawing pictures and so on. They want their children to be always number one in study. According to philosophy, 'every child is a separate identity.' But the parents ignore what their children like or want to do. They only know what they want their children to be. Most of the children might have been harassed during the lockdown by their loving parents. Why do you need English medium schools? Look what happens in India? The people preferred the teaching job in government schools. Those who do not get the chance there, find work in the government aided schools, those who do not find themselves posted anywhere, may be in government or the government aided institutions, they search jobs in English medium schools. So it does not mean that an English medium school means full proof of quality. Only the quality teachers can impart quality education. The government needs to strengthen the quality of education that is imparted in the schools especially those that are run by the governments.

The online learning could have been the first step towards the technology assisted teaching and learning; but the children who were playing together on the same ground while discussing with each other come to know that the School had started online learning which requires the smart phone with an internet connection. One of the boys went back to home. He told his mother that the school has started online learning. So he wanted a Smartphone. His mother said,

"Beta, we are poor. With much difficulty we had this simple phone which helps us to know how about of your married sister. How could I give you the smart phone? When I work for a day we get the meal twice a day. And look now, I lost my work because of the lockdown. Corona has come in our country. Government had given us the cheap grains, so we are able to eat now. Otherwise, we might have to sleep without anything to eat. Leave the thought of that learning. Do not learn like that. I mean we can never buy the smart phone like my mistress has. Sit here near me. I am cooking for us. Till I complete my work, read aloud what is written in your book. Write as good as the alphabets typed in the book. Nobody will dare to fail you. Beta, this is how you can learn. You are born in a poor family. Poor should not think of online learning."

3

It is the best medium of trial that is known as media trial. *Tablighi Markaz Jamaat,* Nizamuddin was criticized for a long time spreading the Corona disease. The Mullah Saad had quarantined himself. His advisors tried their level best to advocate him on the TV channels. On the television, journalists call 4-5 panelists. Out of which half of them talk on the nationalism and issue the certificates of being the terrorists or anti-National. Opposite side use to talk about the constitution, justice, secularism, enquiry, FIR and so on.

Many TV channels had a single handed program to criticize either the opposition or the Muslims and praise the government. Then you will say that media is the fourth pillar of democracy. How dare you to criticize the media? But the situation is quite different. The politics of India is going through a transformation. The journalists praise the government because they want the advertisements from the government for their channels. To run a

TV channel, one needs money. The best medium to earn money is to get the advertisements. If you are in favour of the government, you will get more advertisements. If you talk real or against the government, you will not get the advertisements. Simple matter it is. This is not the only reason as to why the channels talk in favour of the government. Most of the times, the journalist for some years talk in favour of any party like the party leaders or take their side. After some years, they resign their posts and enter in politics to contest the elections or deliver the speeches in the rallies like the actors and actresses.

TV channel had criticized a lot to the Muslims. They were mentioned as the terrorists, anti-National, jihadist and many other terms were being used by the TV channels. Even some politicians said that the Muslims had started the war against our nation by spreading Corona infection. They want to kill all Hindus; so they had gone to each and every corner of India for preaching the principles of Islam and spread the disease. As Maulana Saad had quarantined himself, he had not come out; everybody was talking about the income sources and objectives of the Markaz. But no TV channel was there to ask who had allowed these people in our country? Who had issued visas? Why did the government not taken the necessary action when the first patient was found? Why did no anchor ask the attacking question? Whether the government failed to guess the nature of the calamity?' Why did the police do not take any action against the *Markaz*, though they knew very well that people had gathered there?

The advocates of the *Markaz* had shown the documents in which they had requested the government to help them to send their people back to their home. As soon as the lock down was declared and the transport system was closed, they arranged their own vehicles; but the government did not give its consent. Don't gather together means what? First tell them how to disperse? But here nobody was interested to show the truth. Just they want to make noise and talk of nationalism. Whenever and whoever raise the right questions, his questions are either ignored or is not given enough time. They lead the discussion in the way they want. They have their own agenda. When the number of Corona infected people crossed the number of 20000, everybody stopped talking about *Markaz*, because now people were found infected where there was no chance to blame the Muslims for spreading Corona.

Still the Chief Minister of Uttar Pradesh told the reporters that *Tablighi* will be prosecuted. Then who had stopped him? Time of almost two months had been passed; still no action was taken against anybody. Why? The reason was very simple. There was no evidence which can be proved in the court; because the government was equally responsible for this calamity to take place in India. They were well aware that the court will give clean chit to *Markaz* after looking at the evidences. The government only needs to satisfy the majority of people and thereby hiding their own failures while ruling the country. Decreasing value of rupee in comparison with the dollar, price hikes, decreasing GDP and all other things that they could not complete in the considerable period. Again and again, the *Tablighi* were criticized as anti-National; but it was *Tablighi* who came ahead to donate his blood for the plasma therapy.

The doctors have found plasma therapy treatment to cure the Corona patients. It required the plasma of the person who had already cured of Corona. So the government requested the cured patients to donate blood. The first person who came ahead to donate his blood was a *Tablighi*. On the first day the doctors did his medical check up to point out whether he had any disease. When the reports came he was called on the second day to donate his blood. He very happily donated his blood. The journalists asked him: "How do you feel"? He told that he is ready to donate it again if required. This was a great event. Those who distribute the certificate of nationalism everyday on the television had ignored this *Tablighi*. They did not show this news again and again. Those who showed the news, they showed it in brief. But nobody said that the Muslim had come to help our country; because it was against their agenda. How could they narrate this event in detail? Print media was not also the exception to it. Small news was given regarding this. Only one channel told that in Africa the government had to pay three lakh rupees for one bottle of plasma; but the *Tablighi* had donated the plasma in goodwill. Many thanks to this channel.

4

The Corona was spreading very rapidly. So once the patient was found in any area, the area was identified as containment zone or Hotspot. The area was sealed. People were not allowed to come out of the house. If the patient was found in a society the whole society was sealed. The first thing the administration used to do was to find out the people who were in close contact with the deceased person. Those who were in close contact with the deceased were picked up by the administration and put in the Institutional Quarantine Centers. Quarantine centers consist of the isolation wards where closely associated people with the diseased were put to stop the spread of the disease.

Government was providing the meal and lodging facility as well to the people in contact with the discussed. Those people were not allowed to mix with others. But in some quarantine centres, there were no facilities. No isolation was maintained. The people were behind the net just like pigs captivated in the sty or pen. The compound of this centre had some space at the ground level and the workers in the quarantine centre packets and biscuits through the net. And the people inside tried their level best to get the packets. When the scene was broadcasted on the TV channels, I was shocked. What was the use of those centers then? If the social distance was not maintained, why this centers? It would have been better to ask them to quarantine themselves at home.

In some places, the people were kept in the halls where the marriage ceremonies took place. If people are quarantined at such places, how are we going to face this calamity? Had we accepted our defeat? Most of the people who went to the rural districts from Mumbai were compulsorily quarantined; because it is a nature of man who doesn't allow him to sit quiet. The people do not confine themselves at home, so the government needed to send them in isolation wards; but the isolation wards for those in close contacts with the deceased and others were different. Actually it was a fear of getting infected in those centers because there were many people. The people were living in marriage hall where about ten toilets were there. How can they maintain social distance? Perhaps there was surety of transferring the disease to others. If a single person gets infected, there is a possibility of a whole lot to be infected. If we fight with the problem in this way, would it be possible to overcome this problem? There was a possibility of getting the problem more serious. That is why many people wanted to go back to their native place; because in the shelter places raised by the government distancing could not be maintained.

If we don't want people on the road, we must not extend the lock down; but increase the hours of work. If the people will spend all the time in work, how could they come on the road? If looked around, who are the people you see on the road? Neither the children, the women; nor the old people. Who came on the road then? Only those people who are in habit of going out of the house to work. The government had declared the lock down to save people from Corona; but they are carrying the disease from one place to other and from one person to another. If they had been sent to work, the crowd on the road could have been little bit less. Now they used to go out to see how the situation in the village or city is; or to see whether the police had locked completely or is there a partial lockdown? Some people would visit to know how much crowd is gathered on the road. These people should be punished or may be called Anti National; but who is afraid of the governments?

In some cities in India, the police had decided to put the stamp on the forehead of a person who was breaking the rules of the lock down saying: "I have broken the law of the land. I am an enemy of this country. People in India may go out to see how many people have been stamped by the police." What a great tragedy of our state or country.

5

At the end of the part first of lockdown, a country was divided into three zones: red, orange and green. Maharashtra was also divided into three zones. The division was based on how many cases were found in the district. Right from the first day, the red zones were targeted by sealing the containment zones. In orange zone, where the patients were found very less in number, the administration didn't take care. Many infected people crossed the district borders and entered the orange and green zones. Administration was not so careful; the orange zones became the red zones till the end of lockdown part-II. The same case happened with the green zones. The green zones became orange in some states and red in other states.

Till the end of the period of lockdown part -I, not a single patient was found in many districts in Maharashtra; but those people who came from the cities like Pune and Mumbai changed the colour of their own districts. Green to orange or orange to red. Even the small villages were suffered due to it. At the end of lockdown part-II, the government had given the distribution of the districts again in three zones. Zone wise list of districts were published at the end of lockdown part- II.

Red zone: Mumbai, Pune, Thane, Nagpur, Mumbai Suburban, Nashik, Aurangabad, Yavatmal, Solapur, Akola, Jalgaon, Satara, Dhule, Palghar

Orange zone: Raigad, Ahmednagar, Buldhana, Nandurbar, Kolhapur, Hingoli, Ratnagiri, Jalna, Nanded, Chandrapur, Parbhani, Sangli, Latur, Bhandara, Beed

Green zone: Osmanabad, Washim, Wardha, Gondia, Gadchiroli, Sindhudurg

The list showed how the carelessness of the administrative officers and the citizens made the damage to the state and country as well. In the name of the essential services, people freely moved from here to there. If proper care had been taken, there would have been a good and different picture of the state and country as well. But the number of Corona infection went on increasing rapidly and the lockdown part- III was announced up to 17th May, 2020.

What the country had intended when the first lockdown was declared or before that when the *Janata Curfew* was kept all over the country? It was a dream to control the demon that had come in the form of covid-19 and troubled a lot to the whole world. What happened to the dream that everybody of us had seen?

It is falling into pieces. Completely broken. No use of lock down was visible in the country. If it had shown that there is no use of lockdown, then why did the government extend it more and more? If the lockdown was an answer to the problem, then why did not we succeed? Somewhere there was a mistake. And what we are paying for that mistake? The workers without work were very eager to leave their workplace and go back to their home states. If they had Work, what should they do? Do you expect them to continue their living without work? If there is no work, how can they pay for the rent, pay for the bread and butter? Answer was unknown. Nobody has proper answer for this question. So only stating the extension of lockdown was going on without any achievement.

6

When the first lockdown was declared, it was advised that only those who are infected or are associated with the deceased and the Corona Warriors should use the masks. All other people were not told to use the masks; after all, it was not needed. If the infected takes proper care; there was no fear of its spread. After the end of lockdown part-1, it was recommended that all the people should use masks because everywhere there was a possibility of getting infected. Somewhere, it was reported that some people in Quarantine Centers had run away. Police had filed the FIRs against some people for violating the rules.

When the people started purchasing the masks and sanitizers, there was a shortage of it in the market. All the wine industries started producing sanitizers because the production of wine was stopped. Many women who were in tailoring profession started sewing masks. This was a social service and not a profession. They were working without earning money. They were sewing masks for the police, doctors, nurses and all other Corona Warriors. They had distributed the masks without charge. This was a kind of *sanjivani* or lifesaver for the Corona Warriors, because till this time N95 masks were not given to the Corona Warriors and their life was in danger.

When the institutes where the specially gifted children were living came to know about the scarcity of the masks, they trained those children to sew the masks. Everyday specially gifted children who could not talk or could not listen, started preparing one thousand masks a day. There was no professional attitude. There was love, helping nature and cooperation to the Corona Warriors. The Masks prepared by the specially gifted children were distributed among the police, nurses and all other Corona Warriors. When all the people were locked in their houses, the small children were working hard for the Corona Warriors. This was in the service of the nation. When healthy people were living at home to protect themselves from Corona infection, small and specially gifted children were doing their best to protect the Corona Warriors. The people who were talking of nationalism and patriotism from the sun rise to the midnight on the television hid in their houses to protect themselves.

Not only the disabled children, but also the women having sewing machines started preparing the masks. The cloth they had purchased was used by them to prepare the masks which then were distributed to the police and other Corona Warriors. The children and women are generally treated marginally. They are deprived of their fundamental rights. These people were supporting India through the ways they can. Even the National Service Scheme students prepared the posters advertising what care should be taken to protect oneself from the Corona. The girl students drawn *rangoli* in front of their doors to create awareness among the villagers so that they me be able to save themselves from the infection. Some people were distributing the sanitizers and masks to the poor people and Corona Warriors as well. Some middle class people came together and distributed grocery kit to the poor and needy people. No doubt, some of them were making it an event by taking photographs of the event and making it viral on the social media.

Section III

1

It was a wonderful day. Wonderful means wonderful. The government had allowed the opening of wine shops in all red, orange and green zones. It was said that the economy is in danger; so there is no other way except sale of wine. Wonderful experiences we had today. The journalist was interviewing the person who was present in front of the wine shop.

: How do you feel this day?

: This is really a wonderful day.

: Are you happy?

: Sir, I am very happy today. This is the happiest day.

: Is there any special reason?

: Yes sir, really. I am very happy. The government had paid attention to our problem.

: What problem?

: Sir, I had not drunk for last 40 days. I was not feeling better at home.

: Now the shops are open. What will you say?

: I want to thank the government for opening the wine shops. We had to wait for a long time for this decision.

: How many bottles you are going to purchase?

: Today, I shall buy a dozen.

: A dozen?

: Yah, today I shall drink. Eat mutton and drink wine till I satisfy. And I will sleep for 3 days.

: The shop is not opened yet. How long have you been waiting here?

: Sir, I had been here from 6 a.m. in the morning.

: You came very soon. The shops will open at 10:00 a.m. Don't you know?

: Sir, I know everything; but if I had come at 10:00 a.m., I might have found a long queue. Almost a mile.

: Now you are number one. What will you say?

: Sir, I am the cleverest of all. I focus on my goals. Pursue them with loyalty. So I never loose.

: Yah, I got it. Today also you will win. Best luck. Thank you for talking with us.

Till 10 a.m. all over the country the people were standing in the queues in front of the wine shops. Many of them were very thankful to the government for opening the wine shops. The government ordered to maintain social distancing in wine shops. But what can these people do? They had not taken wine for the last forty days. The TV channels were showing the long queues in front of the wine shops. There was no space for other news. They had not told anything about the migration of workers to their home States and also their sufferings, their problems or their worries. There were long lines in front of the government hospitals for the medical certificate was needed for getting e-Pass to go to their home States.

Everywhere there were queues: in the market, in front of the wine shops or in the government hospitals. And the police had to do the *Lathi* charge to disperse the crowd. When the social distance was not maintained, the wine shops were closed. And the people were forcibly sent to their homes.

People had their own problems; and this was a chance to the doctors to get bribe from these poor people. As the medical certificate was compulsory the doctors from the government hospitals started working for money. It opened a new door for the agents as well. The people had no money to pay for rent of home, to pay the fare of train, to pay for the grains, to pay for the grocery and to pay for the vegetables. And if they had money for all these things why did they want to go back to their native place? They had no source to earn money for their living. The government had allowed them to travel across the states to reach their home; but the central government had said that the respective States or the workers should bear the expenses on travel.

The people coming to get the e-passes had to purchase

the train tickets at first and then they were issued e-passes. The government of Bihar said that the state would not bear the amount of travel. The Government of Uttar Pradesh was not ready to let the people enter in their state. Those people who were born in the state where unable to enter in the state without the permission of the government. A new positive thing happened in politics of the country. When the TV channels told that these people have no money for meals, how could they pay for the rent of the Trains? Then the president of the opposition party declared that their party will pay for the rent of those travelers. The ruling party found the politics in the action of the opposition party. And the opposition party was criticized for doing the politics in such a condition. But this was good politics. Political parties are made for that. No political party can be in politics without doing it. As a result of this, the ruling party had to change their decision and declare that 85% of the total rent will be paid by the central government and 15% will be paid by the state government. It is a good thing that Corona had taught to our politicians. This will definitely be a milestone in the history of Indian politics. The action of the opposition party without any pressure, band or strike made the ruling party to change their decision.

Some people had started going back home walking continuously. Some people chose to go by the bicycles. Some went through the two wheelers. Most of them were stopped on the state borders. These people were requesting the government to allow them to pass through their states; because most of the workers were from Bihar and Uttar Pradesh. They had to cross four to five state borders to enter their own state. Most of them walk in the night because the sun was very hot during the day. In the morning they had to beg for meal and water. They used to walk till the afternoon. If they found any big tree or the closed hotel by the side of the road, they used to take rest in the afternoon. Again in the evening, they had to start their journey. Endless journey it was.

Those illiterate people who do not know Aarogya Setu App or the process to take permission had their own ways to go back to their home. A man had seated two children in a toy car and a string was tied to his bicycle. His wife was seated on the back carriage having a bag hanged on her back. And he became the driver. He had started a journey which may take ten to fifteen days to reach his home. They may not be sure if they will live till they reach home because many people died of the continuous walking or the physical exertion.

Very interesting messages were received on the WhatsApp. The first message said that we generally hate the drunkards, but they should be respected hereafter because they are strengthening the economy of our country. Another message said that if a person entering the wine shop, don't say he is buying wine. Instead say that he is strengthening the economy of our country. The next message said that the name of wine party is changed today. Hereafter it will be known as economy strengthening party.

The Army, Navy and Air Force gave a salute to the Corona Warriors that is the doctors, police, nurses, health assistants and all others participated in the war against Corona. It might have increased the enthusiasm of those Warriors but what do the nation needs now? The nation needs to raise new hospitals. The nation needs to help the poor, the workers, the widows, the handicapped, the hungry, and the needy and so on. What we had become was the follower of events. Every time the government was the organiser of such events; but this time the event of organised by the armed forces. Any event, may be small or big, requires spending money. This was such a time where even the small children had given their savings to the Chief Minister fund or PM CARES fund. Children had given the money that were to be spent on their birthdays; but they had given for the national cause. Some young people married without spending money on the marriage and the same amount was handed over to the government officials. Almost all the government servants had given a day's salary to fight the war against Corona.

And here the government had spent money on giving guard of honour to the corona warriors. The scenery was beautiful. Very beautiful. The flowers were showered like a rain over the Corona Warriors from the sky through the aeroplanes. The people were clapping. In the evening also the ships of Indian Navy were decorated with lights on. So it was a very beautiful scene. Indian Army also did their best with the bands, Rifles, horses and what not? It might have increased the enthusiasm of Corona Warriors but how much money was spent on the event? Here thousands of people cannot book the train tickets to go back to their states. Many do not have money to get the medical certificates. Two quite contradictory situations. At one side the Government does not spend money on the essential services; on the other hand, money is spent on such events.

    This was not enough but the central government asked the state governments to bring their people back to their states by buses. When the states demanded train service to bring back the people from other states, the central government gave its permission. When the question of trains was solved, the question of train tickets came ahead because the respective states were not ready to spend money on train fare. When the people, some people, criticized the decision of guard of honour to the Corona Warriors; the Chief of the Armed Forces said that who criticize the event are intelligent mad people. No doubt, we all agree that the coronas warriors are the best; but those poor workers are also not the worst.

2

When the people who want to cross the borders of the state to reach their home were asked to apply online. The interstate migration was also allowed. Government had appointed the nodal officers in every district who can give permission to the workers, students, tradesman, servants and all other people who were trapped where they were when the lockdown was declared. They had to stay there for forty days without doing anything. They had to wait and wait, and the wait was never-ending. At least, they had good news now. That they will go to their homes, but the problem doesn't end here.

The people were asked to apply online on the given link. Unfortunately, the form was in English. How many workers had taken education and are able to read and fill the form in English? Again it is the state's failure. Many people are illiterate. They even cannot read *devnagri* script. How will they fill the forms in English and again online? The second barrier they had to go through was to produce the medical certificate. Again in queues. Everybody wants to go. Who will help them? Everyone was under tension. It was also listened from some people that the doctors were asking for more money to issue medical fitness certificate. The people did not have money to eat as a result of which they wanted to go back. This was not a happy journey for them. How could these people give money? Most important problem of the people was that it was a compulsory requirement for all to download Arogya Setu App in their mobile so that they could get e-pass. Everybody will agree that many people have the smart phones in their hands; but still there are many people who use the basic models of cell phones. They do not afford purchasing the smart phones. Does the government mean that those people should not go to their homes? Or will they be denied justice only because they are poor or they don't have smart phones? Is there no same law for Indians and Bhartiya?

However, there were some non-government organizations in many cities who supported those people. Many had helped the people to download the Arogya Setu App. Some people helped them to fill the forms online; but there was a big difference in the demand and supply. The suffering people were more in numbers and the helping hands were less in number. The helping organizations were tens in number, the helping people were hundreds in number; but the people who needed help were lakhs in number. How many of them can get the help? And what might have been happening with those helpless people? Will they reach their homes? If no, how long they have to wait to see the lockdown is off?

Really, the government made many mistakes. Firstly, a day's curfew. Secondly, the Government of Maharashtra and Delhi's imposing of the curfew. Thirdly, before the end of the curfew the central government imposed the nationwide lockdown for twenty-one days. It means they had guessed that the lockdown will break the circuit of Corona chain within those three weeks; but their guesses failed. Before the end of this lockdown many state governments imposed the lockdown up to 30th April. Finally, the Government of India extended lockdown up to 3rd May, 2020. The situation of Corona infection had become worst till the end of the second lockdown. The number of Corona infection almost crossed thirty thousand. It means the lockdown had not broken the chain. So the central government again declared the lockdown for the third time for the fourteen days. This time it was up to 17th May, 2020. And nobody in the country knows what will happen on 17th May, 2020. Thank God, the government had given permission to the people to go to their homes. Both intrastate and interstate migration of the people was allowed with pre permission. The state government of Delhi said that revenue collection is decreased up to the ten percent. And the time has come for the state to learn to live with Corona. It is not so difficult to live with Corona. One can change one's lifestyle to protect oneself from the disease. And the best way available was to use masks, maintain the social distance and wash hands with soap or sanitizer. Don't touch your nose, face, mouth or eyes unnecessarily.

If the people follow all these things and start their routine as it was before, Corona cannot perhaps harm us. We can give the example of Japan where people use masks on every day. So they were not suffered from the Corona infection and they did not lock their country. What we have experienced in India was that the chain was not broken and the result was uncontrollable Corona. We are locking our villages, cities, States or Nation. But all the shops must be open for 24 x 7. If this will happen why the people will gather? If they are well sure they will get what they want, they won't be in haste. But due to the fear of the lockdown, when you allow people to go out in a stipulated time, there is a chance to gather crowd. When the city is open for essential services, the crowd is no less than the markets every day. One might feel that there is no fear in the mind of those people regarding Corona. One more thing, we Indians are not made up to live in houses. Those who work in offices, shops, schools, industries and the construction companies, they develop the habit to go out of the house. They cannot be locked at their homes we really want to fight against Corona. If proper care is taken at the workplace, the working class will spend their whole day in work. It will contribute to the GDP of our nation and the people won't find time to gather on the roads that may help to break the chain of Corona infection.

3

By taking permission to cross the state borders, the migrant workers left for their states. Some people, the intra-state migrants, had already crossed the borders of the district by going through the bikes or other means they could use. Some people had entered their districts through the water way. They had travelled through the private boats. Whoever there may be, a man finds solace and peace of mind at home, so everybody wants to reach home. Maybe he is Maharashtrian or he is from other state. The love for home is everywhere. Those people who had come for work and to make their future in Maharashtra from hundreds of miles, have all become restless as and when the lockdown was declared. They feel comfortable here when there is work; but once they lost their jobs, they became restless and became nostalgic. No other thought was in their mind other than going back home. They did not think of the plans they had in their mind when they came to Mumbai, Pune or Nashik. Even the people from rest of the Maharashtra were very eager to go back home. Though the government had made some arrangements of meal and other needs, people could not live like this. Many students, teachers, workers and tourists were ordered to stay where they were. The State Transport was closed, and the airports were sealed, even the district borders were barricaded by the police and were under police observation for 24 x7.

After forty days, the administration gave its consent to the intra-state migration. People had to apply online. They were thousands in numbers. The government declared that the people who were trapped in other districts will be sent to their districts by the State Transport. And the government will bear the expenses on their transport. It was a good decision taken by the state government.

The government quite considerably thought of the problems of the people; but on the other hand, the cases of Corona infected people were increasing rapidly. It has already crossed 16000. If the people were directly sent to their districts, there was a chance of Corona infection; so the proper care was taken. The people were given time for medical check-up. If the person was found medically fit, he would be sent to his district. It was also decided that the people after reaching their districts have to live in the isolation wards; otherwise, there was a chance for the spread of covid-19 infection in the whole village or city.

Most of the people who crossed the borders in illegally

reached directly to their home. They did not quarantine themselves at home. So once they found positive, the people in close contact were found infected. It means if one case is found positive, it was sure that within one or two weeks at least ten new patients will be found positive. Number went on increasing from one to fifteen thousand. Now because it's time to break the chain of infection, the administration had become alert. No doubt, they have some limitations. Many decisions taken on the administrative level also proved to be wrong. But they were working on trial and error method. Now they declared that the shops under the essential services will remain open from 9 a.m. to 7:00 p.m. And the movement of people from 7 p.m. to 7:00 a.m. was strictly prohibited.

The government had to fight on each and every level. They had to think of the revenue as well; so the government levied extra tax on the diesel and petrol. The government also opened the wine shops. The officers working on the administrative level often make severe mistakes. Sometimes we feel that the officer is mad. In the last fortnight, I was happy to know that at one district the teachers were asked to help to seal the district borders because the police force available was not enough. I was overwhelmed with pleasure because of a feeling of happiness to be a part in a war against Corona as a Corona warrior. But today, the government officer on the tehsil level issued an order by which he appointed the senior college teachers to make queues in front of the wine shops. How disgusting it was?

There is a system in India where the people themselves offer parties and bribery very happily to the government officials and police. But there are certain restrictions on the teachers. If he is found near the wine shop he is criticized. It does not require that people find him or catch him Red Handed while drinking wine. His being in the wine shop is enough to say that his character is not good. There are many reasons behind that. We have a long history of the Rishi's and Maharishi's who were given much respect in our country so that the Gurus are expected to behave in good manners. But today this tehsildar had misused his power and issued an order to the teachers to be present in front of the wine shops. He might have been jealous of the teachers. Actually he should have thought many times before issuing those orders. But as he was given the power by law, he misused it. When his decision was criticised on the social media, and some people complain to the Minister, Higher and Technical Education, he ordered the tehsildar to withdraw his decision. Finally, he withdrew the given orders and said that there was no any wrong intention behind it.

After sometime, the teachers shared their views on the social media that it was the conspiracy of the Principal where they were working and the tehsildar who together did this wrong deed. It was a good thing that the Minister helped the teachers and they were saved. Otherwise, they might have been in front of the wine shops.

4

Nineteen people were slept on the railway line and an accident on the railway line. They were working in the Industrial Centre, Jalana and living together like brothers. Due to the Lockdown, they had no work. As they were working in private sector, they became the victim of the principle of no work no pay. They had come from Madhya Pradesh. Having lost their jobs, they had a problem of daily meal. Moreover, they were worried of their relatives. When they came to know that the train will go to Madhya Pradesh from Bhusawal station, they took a firm decision to go to Bhusawal. But it was not so easy. Due to lockdown, the district borders were sealed and nobody was allowed to enter or go out of the district without prior permission. They were supposed to get the e-passes to go to Madhya Pradesh. They had applied for the same last week; but the government of Madhya Pradesh did not respond them in anyway. They wanted to go back, but how could they? They came to know how other people had crossed the district borders not through the main roads but through the subways, through the Hills and rivers; because if they choose the main road the police won't allow anybody to go ahead.

There was a group discussion among them in which everybody shares their ideas. Most of them said that they should leave for their village tomorrow. And it was planned to go by walking up to Bhusawal station. They had their clothes and the Tiffin in their hands. They thought that they should reach Bhusawal by the railway line. There was no fear in their mind because nobody would stop them, so they went on walking and walking. Wherever feeling tired, they used to stop for some time and again start their journey towards Bhusawal. The destination was not so near. It would take some days to reach there. But there was confidence among them. They were the hard workers. That's why they dared to start such a long journey on their feet. And they went on while talking with each other. In the evening, they stopped for some time and took their dinner. As they were very tired, they decided to stop the there. They were talking with each other. While talking, some of them just touched their backs to the ground. Being tired they had sound sleep. They were slept on the railway line because it was the flat space. They had heard that the Railways were not running on the lines. There was no fear in lying on the railway lines; but they did not know that the goods carrier trains were running as usual. We know how speedily these trains run. But these people were not aware of all these things. They didn't know that it will be their last night on the earth.

At night, when all of them were in sound sleep, the goods carrier train arrived very fast which made much difference. It is the difference between life and death. Life is when you are and death is when you were. These people lost their lives due to the train. They were not waiting for this train; they were waiting to get the other train which will take them from Bhusawal to Madhya Pradesh. To reach home was their dream. The goods carrier train came in between them and their dream. The motorman also saw them sleeping on the railway line, he tried to stop the train by using the emergency brakes. Till he stops the train, it had crossed these people. Fourteen people died at the same time, three were injured severely and only two people could save their life because they had slept near the railway line and not on the railway line. When the two people got up, they had a shock. They couldn't believe on their eyes. All their friends had lost their lives. Their body parts were scattered around the railway line. They could do nothing but cry loudly. The railway officials took these two people away from the railway line and gave them water to drink.

Finally the police arrived. They asked those two as to why and where they were going and why they had slept there. Both of them told that they were going back to Madhya Pradesh. In the morning, when everything was visible around, these two people saw that the bodies of their close friends had been broken into pieces. Somewhere the broken legs, somewhere the fingers, somewhere the hands, somewhere the broken head from where the brain had come out. It was a terrible picture. When the news of the death of these people reached Madhya Pradesh, the government declared big package as compensation to the families of the dead. Even the officials had come to visit the place of accident and carry the corpses of the dead by the special aeroplane. Look at the tragedy, when people wanted to go to their home; they had neither got any vehicle nor any facility to reach their home. Once they lost their lives, within half an hour the ambulance was on the spot where they met an accident. Many people along with the police were busy in collecting the body parts of the dead. Once their body parts were collected, their corpses were taken to the Civil Hospital by the special ambulance. Look at the service that is rendered to the dead; transport, economic package, TV coverage and the sympathy at the same time. When people had the problems of their daily meal, nobody cared for them. Once they lost their lives, they became the centre of attention for all the Indians.

5

Corona locked the people inside their homes. Nobody was there to take care of workers. What should they do in such a critical situation? When the lockdown was in the first phase they had taken it very lightly. They thought that the issue will be over in three weeks. And there was also no option available to them without accepting the fact. Having left from their jobs, they had to eat without work or with the favour of the government or the NGOs. They were of the opinion that if they had been informed earlier, they might have gone to their states. But what could have they done there? The governments of their states were unable to provide employment to these people, so they had left their states.

Most of the Maharashtrians and the people from other states in India say that Mumbai does not allow anybody to sleep without food. Nobody dies here without food. Mumbai facilitates everybody to live with self-respect. Work and eat is the basic principle there. Whoever is jobless comes to Mumbai in search of work and lives wherever he can. Maybe on the railway station, maybe on the bus stand, maybe on the footpath. Many people already live in the slums. In a single room of ten by ten, there live four-five families. They use the common toilets. They have to bear all this only to earn their living. Once the person comes to Mumbai, he goes back to his home only to enjoy holidays, to attend the festivals or the marriage ceremonies. Mumbai calls them back. The person once settles in Mumbai, he becomes Mumbaiwala. He may work as sweeper, may work in hotels or can be a seller, selling the toys, clothes, anything. Only the person who has the wish to live his life with self-respect gets settled in Mumbai very easily.

But today what is the picture in Mumbai. Many areas have been identified as containment zones. These areas are locked completely to break the chain of Corona infection. But one area is sealed and the patient is found in the other one. Again lock it completely. Find out the people in close contact with the deceased, move them to the quarantine centres and the deceased to the hospital. All the people are surrounded by the Corona. Everywhere there is a kingdom of fear.

Everybody wants to save himself or herself from Corona; nobody takes the essential care or precaution. Nobody maintains the social distance. So the number went on increasing very rapidly in Mumbai. The government tried its level best to control the infection but it became almost impossible to control the disease.

How many days the people can live in Mumbai without work. Mumbai runs 24 x 7 without a pause for a second. Buses, trains, rickshaws, trucks and all other vehicles run for twenty-four hours. Bus now all the vehicles are parked beside the roads. Even the Rikshawalas are penniless. They have now the problems of money. If you do not have work, how will you get money? But both the stomach and family requires money. If money is not there, how will you continue your life?

The government had no other way than extending the lock down. And continuing lockdown means taking away your jobs, making you penniless, hurling yourself in problems. If you have no job in city, why should you live there? So the people had decided to leave the city. The transport was closed. The trucks were running; but they won't allow the passengers because it was prohibited by law. Those who could go by the trains run by the government went safely. Some of them reached their states by the buses offered to them by the state government. But those who did not found any way to go back home decided to go to their states on their own. Many of them took their rickshaws and started their journey towards Bihar or Uttar Pradesh. So the Mumbai-Agra Highway was jam. Many petrol pumps saw the long lines of rickshaws. The lockdown was declared only to avoid such jams; but the same lockdown became the reason for the jams.

But those who had no rickshaws decided to go by bicycle. The bicycles on the roads were in thousands. And their journey was not so short. They had to cover the distance of a thousand or more kilometers. They were depressed of the joblessness for almost two months, but they had not admitted their defeat. They had not lost their confidence. Some of them took their bicycles for the journey. It was no doubt a big challenge for them, but not unattainable.

6

People in Mumbai, Thane, Pune, Nashik and Aurangabad feared of Covid 19 and its spread. So migrant workers, students and teachers started going back to their villages by crossing the district borders. Most of the out state workers went back by foot, bicycle, bike, rickshaw, bus or train. After the partition of India, Migration of people on such a large scale never took place in India. Even the people from the various districts wanted to go back to their homes. One thing was that they had no work and the second thing that they had guessed that the lockdown will be extended again and again. They had guessed that at least within a month's lockdown, it will be under control; but they lost their hope. Even the Prime Minister had given the hint that the Lockdown Part- 4 will start after 17th May, 2020.

The people, who had stopped at the place where they were when the first lockdown was declared, when they came to know that the lockdown part-IV will be there, could not stop themselves from going back to their homes. They had lost the hope that the disease will be controlled and they could start their work or business when it became clear that it will not end and may be continued for months together. Though the patients were found in the end of the year 2019, it means even after six months; the scientists all over the world had failed to find out the vaccination to protect the people from the disease; so the workers thought that their native place would be good for them and they finally decided to go back to their native districts. Most of them applied for the e-pass. Those who got the bus went to their home by bus.

But all others who did not get E-pass directly took their cars and started their journey towards their home. At some places the police stopped them; but how many people can be stopped? What the police will do? They also feared of infection. So they just send them away. Many people came back in the villages. If these people had not gone in their villages, their villages might have been safe forever. But like the story of a female Monkey, the people entered the village by hook or crook.

The Monkey had a small baby. There was a heavy rainfall in jungle. The water was flowing with force. At some places the water was blocked. The water level continued increasing fast. The female Monkey tried her level best to protect her child by hiding the baby in her arms. She had grabbed her baby close to her stomach. Then the water level increased again; so she took her baby on her back. The rain was falling continuously; then she put her baby on her shoulders. Then the water level came up to her shoulders and she took her baby on her head. Still the water level increased. Finally, the mother worried about her own life as a result of which she placed her baby under her feet to increase her height so that she could save her own life. The story tells that when a life of a person is threatened, he is ready to take other's life.

In the same way, the people from red zone did. When their own lives were threatened, they started leaving their current locations and move towards their native place. People in rural areas were also frightened. Many villagers decided that people from outside would not be allowed to enter the village. They had blocked the roads taking you to the village by placing the boulders and big stones. In most of the villages, the young boys took the wooden sticks in their hands and patrolled themselves day and night to prohibit others from entering in the village. But when it was reported that in emergencies the ambulance cannot enter the village and there was a possibility of danger to the lives of people in village. So they unlocked the roads; but the patrolling was continued.

The Government started issuing e-pass to those who wanted to go to their villages. Even the villagers were worried about their relatives locked in the cities. So they proposed the villagers to take the decision that the people from the cities be allowed to enter the village. Some people opposed the proposal by saying that the care they had taken for the last two months will go in vain. But the people in the cities cannot be left to die. The villagers then took the decision that the people coming from outside will be quarantined in the schools for fourteen days. So many people started coming like flood in villages. Many people stayed in schools. Some people feared that if they live in schools and get infected what is the use of going back to village; so they preferred to stay where they were.

People were very alert. A man came to a nearby village from Mumbai in a tempo which went there to send the vegetables. His brother went on a bike to bring him home. As the news reached the village that the person is coming in the village, the villagers went out of the village. As the person came on the bike, he was kept in the primary school. Unfortunately, within two days, he suffered from severe throat pain. He was coughing continuously. So he was admitted in the hospital and there he was found Corona positive. The villagers were very happy for they kept the decision firmly. It saved the village from destruction. Otherwise, he might have infected at least ten to twenty people in the village. Fortunately, the proper care had saved the village.

The other case in our Tehsil was very sad. A person who was a truck driver had come from Rajasthan. The truck transport was not banned in lockdown stage-II and III. Even interstate. So he had reached Rajasthan and came back to village. He was also asked to live in a school. He lived there, but there gathered his friends. They played cards in the school. Nobody tried to stop it.

After four days, he suffered from cough and throat pain. He was taken to the Civil Hospital and he also found Corona positive. Then the three nearby villages came under pressure; because those who were playing cards in schools belong to the three different villages. So the Administration became alert and all three villages were locked at the same time. The people in close contacts were shifted to the isolation wards and their swabs were sent to the lab. For the next three days, nobody could sleep with comfort. Everybody was anxious to know whether he or she will be the one among the infected or in the close contacts with the infected. When all the close contacts found negative, the villagers could eat a bread of satisfaction.

Though this was the situation in our Tehsil, people were coming to the villages; but they were quarantined in the school. But in a village within the next 2-3 days, the brother of an influential leader was to come. The leader said:

"My brother is coming tomorrow or the day after tomorrow in the village."

"It's good, he is finally coming," said one of the villagers."

"But he won't live in the school."

"Why"? Asked the other one. The dialogue went on.

"He can't live here in this condition."

"We have unanimously resolved to quarantine the people for fourteen days in the school."

"But I won't let him stay here for the safety."

"We have taken the decision for the safety of the village only."

"No facilities are here in the school."

"No, no. Here's everything. The fan is working in the room. Toilet facility is ok. And water tank is always full here. What else do one need"?

"If you want my brother to stay here, he should get a separate toilet and water connection as well."

"How many toilets can we build? The Gram Panchayat has no funds."

"What should be done? I don't know. But I know if my brother is to stay here, I want a separate toilet and water connection also."

"Then ask him to stay where he is; because we have decided. No change."

"He will come. Definitely, he will come. Nobody can stop him from coming here. But if these facilities are not given, he will live in my house. Not in school."

For more than an hour, the discussion went on without any decision; but they had to decide at least something. Discussion resulted in the quarrel. Some people said that if we want to stop quarrel, either his brother will stay in school after he comes; or nobody will be quarantined in the school hereafter. Everybody will be sent to his house. One has to decide how he can maintain the physical distance at family. The decision was resolved and those who were quarantined were released to go to their homes.

7

Many people lived where they were when the lockdown was declared. So we also decided to not to go anywhere because there was no such danger if locked the family inside the home. I was the only person who used to go out to purchase grocery, vegetables or milk. So the family was safe in the home, though it was a rented one. There were two tenants including me. The house was well-furnished home on the ground floor; but for the last five years, the owner had no not lived except for a month when he had come for his son's wedding. All the family had lived there for a month; but once all the religious rites completed, the family shifted back to Mumbai. The other tenant was a worker. There were three members in his family. In lockdown-I, he stayed with us. So there was no tension if his son enters our house or play with my children. But at the end of the first lockdown, he went to his native place. As he was working in the same district, he could easily reach his home. But after some days, his work started and he came back to live near us. We were frightened. We had never allowed our children to go out of the gate, but this family had gone crossing ten villages and coming back after ten to fifteen days by the same route to live with us. We could not stop them. We kept quiet. Now there was a fear of infection. They had gone, lived there and came again. Maybe their son had played with the children of those who had come from Mumbai. If the child or anybody from his family is the carrier of Corona.....

The fear of infection started all this. As and when the child used to ring the bell, we used to take him in but used to ask him to sit away from the children. Then he used to go back. When the children play on the terrace, he used to come; but his parents never tied mask on his face; so my children used to come back. We had to take care for at least fourteen days. Once the period is over, he can do anything. But to complete this period was a difficult task for us. Our love used to attract him in our house; but once he is told to sit at one place, he used to go back. Perhaps, it was an injustice to a small child; but no way was left with us. Before that in twenty-four hours, the child used to be with us at least six to eight hours a day, but now he was not welcomed at my house. In eight days, the family went back to their village and told us that they won't come back till the end of the lockdown. Then we could take rest. Last eight days, there was a tension for all of us. Then we lived for almost fifteen days without tension. But when the Prime Minister gave the hint of lockdown part-IV, the owner of our house came in the night by car from Mumbai. With the sound of car, my wife wake up and told that the family of the owner had come from Mumbai; but I said they won't come.

In the morning when I heard the voice in the ground floor which was locked forever, I called him and asked whether he had come from Mumbai. He said, "Yes" and I was frightened. Further he said that his family would neither come in our gate to switch on the bore well, nor will they come on the terrace. He requested to provide the water. I told him to call as and when they want fresh water. My wife was very anxious. She insisted me to go back to our native place. But I was against that because I was afraid of institutional quarantine system. If we are forced to live in the school where there were people from Pune or Mumbai, there was a surety of infection. Instead, I thought to take proper care here only to protect our family. Is it not always better to be at home then to be in a quarantine centre?

8

Lockdown Part-II was finished. Even the lockdown Part-III came to an end. Only few days were left. Everybody had thought that lockdown may not be extended. Even the TV channels ran the news with the help of resources that there would not be district wise list of red, orange and green zones. But the Containment zones will be remained sealed and in all other areas there will be a permission to live life as before. People will be asked to take proper care to save themselves from Corona. The Prime Minister of India spoke to the citizens of India before the end of lockdown part-III. Everybody was watching his speech with curiosity. It was a question of their life. He said:

> *From the last four months the world is fighting with Corona virus that had caused in the whole world. Some people are fighting to save their lives. Human beings cannot be stopped, broken or defeated. We have to go*

ahead in the fight against Corona following all the rules strictly. The 21st century is India's century is not only our dream but it is our responsibility. If we have to come out of this disaster, we must be self-sufficient. This is an opportunity for our country to develop. When Corona arrived in India, we were not preparing single PPE kit. We wear producing N-95 masks on meagre scale only. Now, there are two lakhs of PPE kits and N-95 masks are produced every day. 'Vasudhaiv Kutumbakam' is our tradition. In this fight of the world with Corona, the Indian medicines had awakened the hope in the world for which each citizen should feel proud of our country. We have the power, means and talent at the same time through which we can prepare the quality products. We have both, the ways to fight and the way to go ahead. I declare the package of Twenty Lakh Crores which is almost 10% of the GDP of India.

He did not forget to say that the development done by Indians in the last six years helped the country to stand still with confidence during the pandemic. What kind of development was done in last six years? Nobody knows. Because we have seen price hikes, decreasing growth rate, loan defaulters leaving India, decreasing value of rupee against Dollar and so on.

He just gave hint that the Fourth Stage of lockdown which is going to start from 18 May 2020 will be different. That he had received some suggestions from the various States. The total guidelines of the lockdown stage 4 will be conveyed to the public before 18 May 2020, he said. He just prepared the Indians to enter in the new stage of lockdown. At the same time he increased the curiosity as to how there will be the next lockdown. Also he did the same thing while declaring the package of Twenty Lakh Crore Rupees. The finance minister will describe in the next few days how the package will be distributed. Who will be the beneficiaries?

The former Finance Minister criticized the Prime Minister's package that was declared to boost the economy as the headline with a Blank Page'. And what was wrong in his criticism. She did not talk a single word on how and when the package reaches the public. Further, the country was waiting and watching his speech to know what he will do for those who had lost their jobs, for those who came back to their home states and for the farmers who could not sale their crops. King is King, after all. It was perhaps a new event for him.

The finance minister gave the details of the distribution of a special package in the next four days. Every day she was on the television channels. But one interesting thing happened in all this. She had declared the package of Three Lakh Crore Rupees to the small scale industries; but the other minister told that the government had not given the bills of those industries of Five Lakh Crore Rupees. He told that if those industries receive their payments, they will be in good condition to run their business. It means the industries required their due amount and not the package. Then the opposition party asked: Who is the lender and who is the borrower here? Whether the government is going to give something to these people?

The fourth was the final day. The distribution of the package of Twenty Lakh Crores had been declared fully. But it was the last day off the lock down Part-III. People were waiting to know how will be the next lock down. The state government already told that the lockdown will be continued in the red zones and in other areas some economic activity can be initiated. But there were no fixed things. The citizens had to wait for the final circular. The central government also called a meeting of its ministers to decide the nature of the lockdown. When the sources failed to guess what will happen, TV channels continued the news that the new guidelines for lockdown Part-IV will reach to us very soon.

Section IV

1

The Prime Minister had declared that the lockdown 4 will be a different one then the previous three phases. It took more time clear the guidelines of lockdown part-4. Till then the Government of Maharashtra, Telangana and Odisha had already extended the lock down. Late on 17th May, 2020, the central government extended the nationwide log down 31st May, 2020. They had given some suggestions. Even interstate bus service was recommended by the central government; but the decision was left to the state governments. Even the government continued to run the trains to send the migrant workers back to their states. The children below 10 years old people were are not allowed to go out of the house.

In some States, the state administration stops the migrant workers. On the state borders they were not allowed to enter in the state. When the journalists asked as to why they are stopped under a hot sun. They had nothing to eat. Even the water was not available. The men, women and small children were only waiting for the approval of the state administration to enter the state. The administration told they will be left by bus to their destination.

People stopped for a long time, when they were tired of hungry waiting, they started agitating. It shows how sensitive administration was towards the public? Again the same issue can be raised. Those people from foreign land where brought by planes with honour and poor Indians left to die. There Was Nobody thinks of those people. No administration, no Judiciary system no media. The Indians are now left in a very new situation. The wine can be sold, but the crops of the farmers would not be sold. Everywhere there were different rules. In some places National Quarantine and in other places home quarantine. Why was not there a one line policy? If the decision is left to the administrative officers, it leads to the corruption. Maharashtra had seen how the Wadhavan family was allowed the travelling from Khandala to Mahabaleshwar.

Now taking into consideration, the guidelines given by the central government, the Government of Maharashtra issued the new guidelines that would be in force from 22nd May, 2020. One thing worth mentioning wasthat the government had created red zone, non-red zone and the containment zones. Some relief was given to the districts other than red zone. Moreover, if any administrative officer wants to issue new guidelines the specified one, read the final approval of the chief secretary, government of Maharashtra. Intra-district bus service allowed means it will enhance the economic activities.

Even the sports complex are the playgrounds remain open provided the social distancing be made properly. No spectators where allowed on the ground. At least the players can practice on the ground. It showed that the government had changed its mind to start at least some activities. Moreover, the government offices with the hundred per cent capacity were allowed in non-red zones. It clearly shows that the government had come on the right track. Even the industries had been running from. All the shops were allowed to open from 9 a.m. To 5:00 p.m. provided that 5 people will not be allowed anywhere.

2

The migrant workers were going to their home States by this or that way. As and when the people reached the border of Uttar Pradesh, police stopped them. The state government had not provided the buses. The leader of opposition party offered 1000 buses for the workers to send their villages. But the state government asked for the fitness certificate, PUC, registration certificate, insurance, etc. of all these buses. Details of 1046 buses handed over to the government. Only 879 documents out of 1046 were the documents of buses. Others were ambulances auto rickshaws. The insurance of140 buses were lapsed. The fitness certificate and Insurance of buses had been lapsed. Only the documents of 582 buses where found correct.

The migrant workers coming from other states had stopped on the borders Uttar Pradesh in thousands. The places where stopped on the border, but the local administration said that. They had not received any orders from the government. The people were expecting the buses even from the state government the state government neither give their own buses 9 had allowed the basis offered by the opposition party. The government was finding faults in the documents submitted by the opposition.

Dear all the discussion on the TV channel where an expert told that if the central government had Run 10000 trains within a day or two all the workers will have been sent to their villages. Also told that Rs. One Thousand Crore out of Rs. Thirty Thousand Crore's package had been utilized on the Migration of workers,. There was no need for the workers to go under tension payment is organising events for many days. Every day the government wants the heading on the TV channels and newspapers, 'Two trains departed from this state.''Three trains departed from that state' and so on. Also the central government could have taken the decision that will be dropped at the nearest railway station and all the state governments must deploy their buses to help the people to reach their villages. But the central government was also not serious.

There was a rule which said that the approval of the state government was needed for the train from which state will itdepart and to the state where it will reach. But that was not needed. Actually, many times if the state governments take any decision, government do not listen to what the state assembly say. But now in the name of the state approval, the central government was playing with the lives of the people. The people gathered near the railway station were being beaten by the police.

If any state government finds politics is the opposition party comes ahead; it is the duty of the ruling government take the necessary steps as much as they are needed. Party should not give a chance to the opposition party to do politics. If the people in politics do not do the politics, what else should they do? Same thing had happened in almost all the States. Even the experience of intrastate workers was also the same. Everywhere there was a kingdom of fear, problems and injustice.

3

The three phases of lockdown came to an end; but my native Tehsil was quite away from Corona infection. The people from Pune and Mumbai were put in the institutional Quarantine centre. I had not gone there only because of this. If the villagers had allowed living in the farmhouse, I would have gone. But I feared of infection in the institutional Quarantine centre, so I left the thought. But the people were coming thousands from Pune and Mumbai. Even the guests from the Metropolitan cities started coming to our Tehsil for it was secure. The shops were within 2 days; but a bad thing happened. Corona entered our village.

The Grandmother along with her granddaughter had come to our Village in her daughter in laws maternal home. As there was a rule of institutional current in system, her brother-in-law put her in the field 100 *Bihari* workers were living with their families. Stayed there for 2 days; nearby villages complained and demanded FIR to the Quarantine centre. The woman was shifted to the quarantine centre. Within two days she was taken to brother in laws home instead of in the quarantine centre. Today's the woman suffered from throat pain; so her brother-in-law shifted her to the quarantine Centre again. She became very serious there. So she was taken to the local doctors. First doctor guessed of Corona infection, instead of taking her to the government Hospital, she was taken to the second doctor. He also diagnosed the same; birthday brother-in-law was not satisfied with the diagnosis of these doctors. He again took her to the third one. And also recommended to admit her in the Civil Hospital, woman was brought back to the Quarantine centre. The officials present over there were informed about her health. So they called an ambulance. The woman was being taken to the district hospital. She was on the stretcher in the ambulance. After four kilometers run of ambulance, she became unconscious. And fail down in the ambulance her brother in law asked them to the workers to pick her up and put her on the stretcher. She was almost died, but her death was not declared yet. She was taken to the district Civil Hospital where she was declared dead. But as the symptoms she had soon were Covid-19, her swab was taken for testing. It took 15 hours for the reports to come. Till then the whole village was under pressure. Everybody was feared. Many people worshipped the Goddess Yamai man should not be found Corona positive so that the village will be safe forever. But no prayer could come for help and finally she was declared Corona positive. A big headline in the newspaper occurred: mother in-law hurled the daughter-in-law's maternal village in danger. Really she had brought with her from Mumbai to our Village. The heart beats of all the villages where stopped for a while.

The brother-in-law of the dead was in contact with 700 people. How many people have come in contact with those 700 people? Everywhere there were despair discussions. Everybody was sure that some people will be found positive in our village; but how many? Nobody knows. In ones, in tens, in hundreds or what? When I talk with my father, he said that the whole village was sealed. Days and surrounding twelve *wadis* were sealed. Even the small lens where blocked. Thanks used to know the numbers of Corona infected people. I said that people should leave where they are. The changed the place Corona came to our Village. Now I came to know as two why my father did not ask me in last two months as to when I am visiting them. Late Night, I read the news on daily hunt and came to know that only 6 years old girl found Corona positive. Three reports of close relatives were found negative. The people in the village became very happy. After all, the village was saved from destruction. So do 700 people in contacts happy, but the happiness more time. Doctor came forward and said that do the chain reports of those closed are found negative, we have to wait for few more days; because the test negative doesn't mean that they are negative. The Mummy found Corona positive in the next few days; so everybody in close contacts or others contain themselves for the next fourteen days without fail. Otherwise, anything can happen. In this case, three doctors were also quarantined. Many people went to stay in the fields to avoid infection to their family.

4

One day my sister's son-in-laws blood pressure increased hands he was admitted to the hospital. Even the sugar was found in his urine. The doctor advised to shift him to the multispecialty hospital so that she could be treated further. My sister's son is young and energetic. He accompanied his brother-in- law. After 2 days of treatment the doctor advised to shift the patient to Baramati for angiography. He doubted that there may be blockages in the blood veins.

As per the direction of the doctor, the patient was shifted to Baramati where the doctors there declared that there are two blockages in his body. So angioplasty was needed in urgency. My sister's son in law's close relatives told that nothing had happened to him. Bring him back. Once the Corona ends, we shall treat him further. We can't come to the hospital in such a situation. But my sister's son was very firm. He decided to care his brother-in-law as early as possible. Firstly, he asked the doctor, can the operation be done after a month or two; but the doctor said that it is necessary to do it at the earliest. "If you want to wait for a month or two, you can. But the responsibility will be yours," said the doctor. So my nephew came to know that it needs to be done in urgency. So he went back to home and submitted the documents on the next day in the morning. The government spends money on such surgeries of poor people. Illness is not one's belonging. Anybody can get ill. But when our close relative suffers from any disease, we become very sensitive. Otherwise, we have heard many stories of people who met an accident on the road; but nobody helps them. Nobody gives water to the person in such a critical time. Nobody informed the police. If we are in the queue in OPD and if any emergency patient directly goes to the doctor, we feel jealous of him. But when our close relative is serious, the doctor should treat him or her in priority. This is a human nature.

Now look at the doctors, when were reach the hospital in hurry without wasting a minute, the compounder or the nurse ask us to sit waiting outside till the doctor comes. We approach again and again to the nurse and ask her to call the doctor. We request for to tell the doctor that my so and so is very serious. But neither the doctor nor any health assistant staff is serious like us; because seriousness, injuries, pains and the diseases are common for them. They meet only the serious patients. So they develop their personality in the way that they don't involve in the pains of the patient, because it is their profession. They do all that for earning money. If a poor person goes there, will they treat him? No, definitely not.

The greatness of mind belongs to the farmers only. Whoever comes to their field, they welcome him and ask him to test whatever he had grown in the field. If there's a same case of grocer, tradesman, doctor, chemist or any such profession? The answer is not. Even these people have fixed rates. If you are there for a surgery, there is a fix amount you are supposed to pay. But the case of a farmer is different; if a person comes to his field, he does everything in charity. So he is poor and all others rich. Then the question arises as to why the doctor was in Haste to do the angioplasty surgery. The reason is very simple. He knew it very well that the government will pay for it. Hundred percent payment. If the person goes to other Hospital, it's the loss of his business. So they welcome the patients to increase their business. Let it be. But the government approval for the surgery was sought within 36 hours and it was done. I was supposed to be there; but I could not due to the lockdown. When the patient's documents were submitted for approval, my sister's mother in law died. So my nephew need to go back home. He went back, did everything required for the funeral and went back to the hospital to take care of his brother-in-law. He managed everything like an expert. It was a matter of pride for me to have such a nephew.

5

The issue of Gujarat went into the court. Ahmedabad, a city in Gujarat, came into news when the Ahmedabad Medical Association went to the court. This was not the only case of Ahmedabad but of whole Gujarat. And it was doubted there were many people having the symptoms of Corona, what the state government had the policy of 'no test no infection'. The government should control the tests to show the less number of Corona positive people to the world. Many patients admitted in many private and non covid hospitals having the Corona symptoms. Government did not test this patience only to show the small number of Corona infection.

There was a tweet by news agency that was quote of what Dr. Vasant Patel, CEO, Dhwani Hospital and Ahmedabad Nursing Home Assoc. Executive Committee Member.

In Gujarat, particularly Ahmedabad, pvt doctors in non- Covid hospitals get many patients with COVID-19 symptoms. Guard govt has no policy to test who will feel might be infected.

Dr. Vasant Patel further said:

As per ICMR, before any surgery COVID-19 test is compulsory. But Gujarat government is taking COVID tests very lightly and why they are doing lesser number of tests is still not understood by people and doctors.

There was news that a woman named Shantabai Shah Ahmedabad was admitted to the Covid Hospital. She was 92 years old. She had a fever and breathing problem on 21st May, 2020. Her son Vijay Bhai also was admitted in the hospital for he had shown the same symptoms. The dangerous thing was that no one was tested whether they were covid positive or not. Even the Shaha family also accused the state government and blamed the state government whether they are not testing numbers. The family father said that no one would know why she was dead.

The state government had private labs for Corona testing. the private Labs need to take permission of the state government. It was said that if more and more tests are done, almost 70% people will found coroner positive. Even the High Court said that to ban private labs for from Corona testing is not good. According to Gujarat government only 5,000 tests were done 17th to 24th may 2020. On 25th May only 3492 and on 26th May, 2020, 2952 tests were done. Even the opposition party criticized ruling government for hiding the number of Corona positive cases. Even the private doctors complained that from private Labs reports come very soon; what the government did not allow them to test. And the reports from the government Labs very late. So even the health of the doctors is also in danger. If the reports come late, cannot get the right treatment and even the doctors need to Quarantine.

When one lakh sixty thousand people found Corona positive in India, it was reported that almost 70% cases where found in thirteen cities namely Delhi, Mumbai, Ahmedabad, Indore, Kolkata, Hyderabad, Jaipur, Jodhpur, Chennai, Thane, Pune, Chengalpattu and Thiruvallur. So it was clear that the next lockdown part- 5 it will be extended concentrate on these thirteen cities.

6

On 31st May 2020, the lockdown part 4 was to end; but the central government declared the lockdown part 5 up to 30th June, 2020. The central government had taken the suggestions and recommendations from the state and union territories governments regarding the extension of lock down. For the first time the central government used the word ' unlock 1' instead of lockdown. It was the start of the process of unlocking. The government directed that along with initiation of economic activities will be given in all other zones accept the containment zone.

It was a parody bat that the unlock one was from 1st June to 30th June 2020; according to it religious places, hotels, restaurants, and other Hospitality Services, shopping centers et cetera will be opened. Provided this should follow the terms and conditions the central government will declare the guidelines regarding this very soon, it was said. In lockdown four, the night curfew was from 7 p.m. To 7:00 a.m. in the Country; but now the night curfew will be from 9 p.m. To 5:00 a.m., but the central government said that the decision regarding schools, colleges, Educational Institutes; coaching classes will be taken in July after considering the situation many good things were in this proposal. There was a provision of penalty for those speaking in public places the ban on international airports was continued. Metro services, theatres, gym, swimming pools, bar, and entertainment parks were restricted as before. Old people above the age of 65, pregnant women and children below 10 years where advice to stay at home. Interstate and intrastate travel would not require e pass after this. Decision was left to the state government whether to allow people to travel or not. Show the people have to wait for the guidelines of the state governments. All these things will be done in non-red zones only.

It was also said that the containment zones should be focused. The major focus should be on contact tracing and proper treatment so that the disease may be controlled. It shows that had decided to give a strong relief Indians from the lockdown.

Before the guidelines of the central government came, the state governments like Punjab, Odisha and Karnataka extended the lockdown in their respective States. It clearly states that the state governments where still not ready to take the risk till the date they have a fear of breed of Corona in their states. And every state their level best from this calamity. Answer to this 'Unlock 1', the State Government of Maharashtra are used the word ' Mission begin again'. The government offices were opened in the red zones. Many private offices and industries were allowed to start allowing ten per cent or ten workers. Still many industrialists were not happy because they demanded that at least 40 to 50 people should be allowed at workplace. New life had already started. Do the central government had said that there was no need for e-pass to travel anywhere, the state government only allowed the people to travel inter-district in Mumbai, Thane, Palghar only. The State Government of Maharashtra told that the inter district movement of people would be possible only after permission as before.

The Government of Maharashtra also declared that there would be no college or university examinations. The students will get average marks. The decision has been taken after the consultation with the vice chancellors, the educationists, teachers, students and parents as well. To save the students from corona infection, the government had cancelled the examinations. But the chancellor of all universities in Maharashtra, the Governor said that examinations cannot be cancelled. The state government has no right to take such adverse decision. As a result of which again there was confusion among the students and parents whether the examinations will be held or not. The matter was then taken to the court. One more thing was that the first and second year students were allowed to carry forward in the next class. Even the Secondary School Board results were declared. It attracted the

Management to collect money in the form of admission fee. Many institutions started online admission; but those institutes who were taking extra fees from the students made it mandatory to pay offline only. Within two to three days, I received the notice on the WhatsApp from my college to be present in the college. Then came Unlock-2 and Unlock-3 also. But the spread of Corona was not in control; still the life was on the way to normalcy. Four months before five cases meant a lot and now five thousand cases doesn't mean anything. The fear had lost now from the minds and the reason was not that the vaccine was found but the struggle of life had become more and more hard.

ABOUT THE AUTHOR

Satish Saykar is an Associate Professor having sixteen years of teaching experience at UG and PG in English Language and Literature in India. He is a creative writer, translator, literary critic and social activist. He had completed his Ph.D. from Shivaji University, Kolhapur in Literature.

Made in the USA
Middletown, DE
03 July 2021